SciFi Fairy Tale Retelling

Aurelia Skye

Cover design by Amourisa Design
Template by Jacqueline Sweet
Edited by T.K. and J.D.

ISBN: 9781723943317

If you think you know the story of "Peter Pan," think again.

Wendy Darling is a disgruntled employee at Lost Boys Clubhouse on planet Neverland and technically involved with Peter Pan, but he's too busy for her and always flirting with Tink. He's also totally immature and refuses to grow up, so that's why she's leaving him. The arrival of James Hook, in search of something Pan stole from him, derails her plans to return to New London when he kidnaps her and takes her aboard the *Jolly Roger*. As they set off on an adventure that spans the galaxy while evading Admiral Croc, who's on James's tail, Wendy soon realizes she doesn't need a boy when she can have a man.

PROLOGUE

WENDY DARLING HAD REACHED HER LIMIT WITH Peter Pan's bullshit. She could barely remember the younger, more naïve version of herself who had been sweet-talked and charmed by Peter just eight months before. She'd left the colony of New London with barely a backward glance and hadn't even looked out the windows of Peter's ship, the *Pixie Dust*, to glance back at planet Nexa, which had been her home for most of her life.

Now, here she was on Neverland, and she'd discovered Peter was as charming and funny as could be, but he was also irresponsible and careless with other people's feelings and emotions. She was sick of cleaning up after him and his crew, and having the job of bartender at the Lost Boys Clubhouse certainly wasn't a dream come true. It would've been tolerable if Peter had been the man she expected, but he was neglectful and forgetful, and she'd had enough.

With those thoughts firmly in mind, she carried her bag from the room she shared with Peter above his bar, though there wasn't much sharing involved these days. She was busy working in the bar, and he was often busy doing whatever it was he did with his crew of irresponsible men, who were just as immature as he was.

She hefted her bag down the stairs, sliding past Tink Rabelle in the process. Tink glared at her, and Wendy glared right back at the Faetian. She had faintly green skin, a pixie cut with silvery white hair, pointed ears, and stunning features. Everything was perfect about her, including the level of bitchiness. Tink was a perfect bitch, and since she was the only other woman on Neverland that Wendy had seen, at least on a regular basis, she was another reason to leave.

She reached the bottom of the stairs. Getting to the exit required passing Peter's usual table in the corner. He was whispering with Kubrick, and she overheard Peter say the word *traitor* as she walked by. She stiffened and glared at him, at first thinking he was addressing her, but he was still looking at his best friend, and they were clearly discussing something unrelated to her. Peter didn't even glance at her.

She huffed on past and stepped outside, waiting for the transport ship. She'd gotten hold of one with her radio hours before and had been lucky enough to find a position as a dishwasher on a cargo ship in exchange for working her way back to the New London colony. The

Wasp would have to make its way through Neverland's security system, but it should be there imminently.

She placed her bag on the dusty ground and sat on top of it to wait. It was almost a shock when Peter came out a few minutes later, since she had genuinely assumed he hadn't seen her go by. She didn't look at him as he came to stand beside her, not wanting to be swayed by the perfection of his Faetian features. Like Tink, he was a pale green color, but that somehow managed to be vibrant and exciting on him. His hair was a darker blond than Tink's, but in a similar pixie cut as well that framed and showed off his pointed ears.

"What's going on, Wendy?" asked Peter.

She still didn't look at him as she stared upward, hoping for some sign of the cargo freighter whose captain she had been in contact with earlier. "I'm leaving."

"Going back to visit your brothers and grandmother?"

She shrugged a shoulder, honestly sort of surprised that Peter remembered she had family, and how they were related to her. He seemed to have lost interest in her practically from the moment she arrived on Neverland and agreed to share his bed. "I'm going home." Not that New London actually felt like home. The only place she could ever recall feeling like home was planet A28Z, where she had lived for three happy years with her parents, little brothers, and grandmother as her parents worked with the terraforming corporation to transform it to Coalition standards. That was before the Krolilans destroyed the planet, and her parents hadn't managed to escape along with Wendy, Mikey, Johnny, and Nana.

"When will you be back? I'll get Tink to watch after the bar for a bit, but I need to know—"

"Never," said Wendy vehemently.

Peter stood there for a moment, looking surprised. "Why?"

She rolled her eyes and huffed a breath as she looked at him for the first time. "How can you even ask me that? We don't have a relationship. We're practically roommates, and I end up doing all the work around here. I had enough of the mothering thing watching after my brothers when we returned to New London after my parents' death. I didn't come here to babysit you and your crew of reprobates."

Peter blinked, and then he knelt down beside Wendy, looking earnest. "I'm sorry I've been distracted. I didn't tell you this, but at least one or two crewmembers have been plotting against me. They're trying to steal something really important, the kind of thing that makes a difference between owning your own backwater planet at the edge of Coalition space and of owning an entire solar system at the center of the galaxy."

Wendy somehow managed to keep from rolling her eyes. Peter was full of big dreams and big talk, but she saw little evidence that he could deliver. "How unfortunate for you. I'll be one less thing on your mind." Not that she was probably ever on his mind these days, unless he needed a drink or wanted a favor.

"No, don't leave me. I can't go on without you, Wendy." He grabbed her hands, and he seemed sincere. "Things are going to change around here." He leaned closer to whisper, "I know who the traitors are. Once I deal with them, I'm going to have a lot more time for you again. It will be just like it was in the beginning. I promise."

She looked at him with skepticism. "I'd like to believe that, but…" She trailed off with a shrug.

He frowned for a moment, as though thinking deeply about something. Then he reached into his pocket and pulled out a bracelet that Wendy had seen once or twice before, but never on his wrist. To her knowledge, he never took it off his person, so it was a surprise when he opened the clasp and started to slide it on her wrist. She froze, staring at it. "What are you doing?"

"It will be safe with you. This bracelet means the world to me. It has... Well, it's just very important. Knowing you're wearing it will make me feel better, and I hope it'll reassure you that I'm serious."

Wendy didn't keep protesting as he slid it onto her wrist. "I don't know. I have a job worked out the will take me back to New London in a matter of months. If I give up that opportunity, I don't know when I'll have a chance to leave again."

Peter literally crossed his heart with his index finger. "I promise that if you're not happy in a few weeks, I'll take you home myself. I'm just asking for you to give me one more chance, babe. I love you."

There was a time when hearing those words from him would've made her heart melt, but they did barely anything to warm her now. But the bracelet was a big gesture, and she wanted to believe that she hadn't spent the last eight months of her life wasting it by investing in a relationship that was never going to go anywhere. With a hesitant nod, she bit her lower lip before saying, "Okay. I'll stay for a little while longer."

"Thank you for giving me another chance." As he spoke, he pressed a button on the bracelet. It hummed for a moment before getting warm and almost burning her wrist as it flashed gold twice before returning to normal. "All locked."

Wendy scowled. "What are you talking about? Is this some kind of device to keep me locked up?"

Peter laughed. "What an imagination. No. I simply keyed it to your DNA. Some of my associates aren't as trustworthy as I'd like, and I don't want you wearing a bracelet they can easy easily steal when it means so much to me. As do you," he tacked on hastily.

Considering some of the behavior she'd seen during her short tenure as head bartender at the Lost Boys Clubhouse on Neverland, she could certainly believe his friends and associates weren't the most trustworthy. It made sense that he'd want to safeguard the bracelet, and it clearly meant a lot to him. "Was it your mother's or something?"

His face tightened for a moment, but then he shrugged. "Something like that. As I told you when we first met, my parents aren't in my life. They abandoned me at an orphanage, so I have no idea about them or my history."

The way his lower lip wobbled caused Wendy's heart to melt, and she couldn't help reaching out to place a palm against his cheek. He gave her a stoic smile, and she leaned forward to kiss him on the mouth. There weren't fireworks like she'd read about in books, but they'd never been there. It was more of a safe and steady kiss, with a component of sweetness that won her over and kept her returning, where passion might quickly burn and fade away.

Before she had a chance to see if the passion could at least flare, he eased away. "I have traitors to deal with, and you have a ride to cancel, don't you?" His eyes were pleading.

With a small sigh, Wendy nodded and watched Peter walk away a moment later. She still wasn't sure if she was making the right decision, but she had agreed to stay for at least a few more weeks. With that in mind, she used her comm to send a message to the captain of the cargo ship to let him know she was no longer planning to leave Neverland. Yet.

1

WENDY woke alone, which was something she'd become accustomed to almost immediately after arriving in Neverland. She tried not to take it as an omen of having made the wrong decision, since she knew he had been busy dealing with the traitors in his crew the previous evening.

Instead, she went about her day, quickly bathing and dressing before heading downstairs to open the bar—not that it officially ever closed. She worked when she was awake until she felt like going to bed, and then they helped themselves afterward. She made a mental note to check the inventory again as she entered the main area of the bar.

There was a somberness in the air that took her by surprise, and she saw more than one long face as she looked around. "Who died?" she asked cheerfully, trying to elicit a few smiles. Instead, her comment made several people wince. She was surprised when Tink smirked at her before pointing to the front of the bar. Wendy wasn't certain if that was an invitation for her to leave, but she was sure Tink was sorry that she hadn't gone the day before.

Curiosity got the better of her, so she walked across the bar and pushed through the swinging doors to step outside. Immediately, she gasped and took a step back, bouncing into one of the wooden doors. Her stomach heaved, and she barely bit down the surge of nausea as she saw two familiar heads resting on pikes in front of the bar.

Tootles and Curly, who had been regular drinking buddies of Peter's, and also manned his ship when he took the *Pixie Dust* on whatever shady mission he was undertaking at the moment, adorned matching poles. Their heads were all that remained, and Curly's eyes had closed, but Tootles's remained wide-open, and his expression was forever frozen in a horrified scream.

"Snitches don't get stitches," said Peter with a high-pitched laugh from behind her. "They just bleed."

Wendy barely swallowed the nausea and turned to face him. "What?"

"They're the snitches, or in this case, the plotters, so they don't get stitches to fix them up. I took care of the problem, as you can see. I got right to the root of it and cut it out." He giggled again.

She winced at his sensitivity. Wendy wasn't particularly close to either Tootles or Curly, but she'd serve them drinks and listened to their stories long enough to know something about both of them, so it was upsetting to see them as they were. "Are you the one who did the actual cutting, Peter?"

All signs of amusement faded from his delicate, precise features. "I sure was. Don't cross Peter Pan if you want to live to tell the tale."

She nodded and hurried back into the bar, uncertain if he was simply giving her an answer, or if there was something more to it—something like a threat, which made her tremble in spite of herself. Would he consider it crossing him if she left? She wanted to pretend like she could stay, that they could be happy again, but deep in her heart, she already knew she was going to be leaving at some point. Peter wasn't who she thought he was, and perhaps he had never been the man she'd once believed him to be.

CHAPTER ONE

Three months later.

WENDY TOOK ONE LOOK AT THE OVERFLOWING SINK filled with shot glasses and appetizer plates before moving her gaze to the two bus trays, both heaped high with dirty dishes as well. There was a huge stack of dirty bar towels flowing out of the bin, and something sticky on the floor caught her foot with each step she took. She was livid   at   the   state   of   the place, since it had been not quite spotless, but certainly far more under control, before she went to bed the previous evening.

She started to march into the bar, but froze when she saw the door to the supply room open. She detoured to that area and stumbled to a halt when she saw only one shelf of liquor remaining. Peter and his crew could go through quite a quantity every week, but half the time there was no money to reorder, since Peter let his friends drink for free. How was she supposed to make this amount last with the swine that never seemed to leave the Lost Boys?

She marched through to the bar, hands on her hips, and raised her voice to get everyone's attention. "If you want to keep drinking, you need to settle all your tabs now. I'm tired of fronting you slobs and cleaning up after you. I'm not your damn mother."

Kubrick frowned at her. "Peter's never asked me to pay. He's me best mate."

A few other joined in that chorus, and Wendy glared at each of them. "You can't drink for free, because there's no money to replace the alcohol. It's a simple fact of doing business. You have to have money to pay for the suppliers, so you have something to sell. That's why you all have to settle your tabs today."

"I don't even know what my tab is. There's that, innit?" called a Faetian from the corner. He was fairly plump for the species, and he'd clearly enjoyed more than a few glasses of Peter's special house brew that he called Tiger Lily.

"Fortunately for you all, I've been keeping track." Wendy glared at them all again as Peter walked up to her. She braced herself for a fight.

"Relax, babe. These are friends, and we're not going to charge our friends."

She rolled her eyes. "They're *your* friends, and as I was trying to explain to them, if you don't have money to resupply, nobody drinks, let alone for free." She wasn't certain why she cared, because it made her life easier if all the drunks left the bar. Perhaps she was simply trying to teach them all a life lesson about supply and demand, or give them a kick in the ass toward personal responsibility. Whatever she was doing, it was clearly a losing battle if Peter wasn't on her side.

"It's not a problem. We're going out on a job in couple of days, and I'll make sure we raid some stock from somewhere. We'll all continue to drink, and for free," he announced with a loud shout that was met with a chorus of cheers.

Wendy shook her head and took off the apron she had just donned. Why was she still wasting her time with this when all she wanted to do was escape? Three months had changed nothing, and Peter was the same careless, superficially charming, and inconsiderate boy he'd been the day he gave her the bracelet. He still flirted shamelessly with Tink, and he still took Wendy for granted. She was done trying to keep his business together or clean up his messes.

As she slipped away from Peter and behind the bar to head out for a breath of fresh air, Tink blocked her path. The blonde Faetian had a pleased grin on her face. "He doesn't love you, you know? He never did."

Wendy rolled her eyes again. "Like I care. He obviously doesn't love you either, Tink, or he wouldn't treat you like one of the boys." *When he isn't busy flirting with you to make me jealous.* She couldn't prove it, but suspected Peter's feigned interest in Tink was to annoy Wendy and/or to ensure Tink stayed around, since she was one of the best safecrackers, as Peter liked to brag.

Tink scowled. "He and I were together for twenty years."

"Yeah, when you are both young. What were you, seventy?" That was young by Faetian standards. "And he grew tired of you after twenty years. Personally, I grow tired of you after twenty seconds."

She didn't bother to try to push her

way past Tink. Wendy veered away from her to take the steps from the bar to upstairs, intent on heading to the room she shared with Peter. She was going to move her things into one of the smaller rooms that he made available for his drunk friends, also usually without a charge. She wasn't certain how, but she was going to find a way off Neverland as soon as she could.

She'd barely taken the first stair when the proximity alert sounded, and red lights flashed all over the room. They would flash in any building on the planet, which was composed of a single large island surrounded by a choppy ocean that was never suitable for swimming.

"Look alive, lads," called Peter. "We have an intruder."

Wendy turned to face the large vid screen that had previously revealed only the vast waters covering Neverland, but now showed a red and black ship streaking through the sky. It seemed to easily evade all of Peter's countermeasures, including surface-to-air missiles, and as she heard the roar of the engine from the ship setting down outside the bar, she found herself silently cheering for whomever was invading Neverland. They couldn't be any worse than Peter and his useless group of Lost Boys. They might even offer a way off the planet.

The Lost Boys scattered in various directions. Some of them simply disappeared through the nearest exits, or broke through a window. There were a few, including Kubrick, who stayed behind to stand with Peter.

They all had sensible choices for defense with their laser rifles, but Peter reached for the laser sword sitting in the scabbard he'd left at his table. It was the silliest affectation, and even under the circumstances, she couldn't stifle a giggle at seeing him with the sword that was little more than the length of his forearm. He moved like a ballet dancer about to perform, and she hoped he was going to get his ass kicked.

There was some fighting outside, but she couldn't see the initial scuffle, since the vid screen view hadn't changed. All she knew was there were people coming, and she could hear boots on the steps outside the swinging doors a moment later. After that, one of the doors swung open to crash violently against the wall, and the light filtering into the previously darkened interior served as a backdrop to highlight the intruder.

Wendy couldn't make out his facial features, but he was tall and broad-shouldered, with lean hips, and what appeared to be muscular legs in tight-fitting pants. When he stepped inside, and her eyes adjusted to the sudden intensity of the light that was no longer framing him, she could see his features. He would've been classically handsome, with high cheekbones, a straight nose, and firm lips, had it not been for the large scar marring the left side of his face and cutting through his eye.

Clearly, that injury had cost him the original eye, because now a light blue eye that was clearly cybernetic, with a flickering red light instead of a pupil, stared out instead. That eye seemed to miss nothing in the room, and the newcomer swaggered in with confidence despite the laser guns pointed in his direction. Others followed him, and it was quickly obvious Peter and his Lost Boys were outnumbered.

Wendy re-counted, realizing they weren't outnumbered after all. The man who'd entered had only four backing him up, where seven others stood behind Peter, but the four who'd come with him seemed far more dangerous and competent than the seven weaklings who stood behind Peter, almost all with their gun hands shaking.

"What are you doing here, Hook?" asked Peter with false bravado. His voice was trembling, making it hard to pull it off.

"You know why I'm here, Pan. You

double-crossed me, and I've come for it."

"It took you long enough," said Kubrick with a hint of snark that was ruined by the way his hand trembled as he tried to point the gun at one of the people behind Hook.

"You've done a good job hiding your coordinates and obscuring the existence of this place, but you should know better than anyone how determined I am to find you, Pan." Hook addressed the words to Peter rather than Kubrick. "Did you really think you could hide from me forever?"

Peter didn't bother to answer. He simply thrust a sword forward with a challenging air. "You'll never get it from me."

Wendy almost giggled again at how ridiculous Peter looked with his sword, especially when the man identified as Hook eyed it with chagrin for a moment before turning to face one of the men behind him. He clearly trusted his companions to have his back if he would turn it toward Peter and the others for even a moment. "Turley, I'll have your sword please."

"Yes, Captain." The man identified as Turley was tall and broad, with swarthy skin and beautifully contrasting silver hair that he kept combed back and confined with a synth-leather thong. He didn't hesitate to offer his sword, and this was a real sword. It was long and lethal-looking even before Hook flipped a button that made it glow with the hum of electricity and gave it a menacing look that Peter's little laser sword couldn't hope to achieve.

Wendy saw movement from the corner of her eye and looked at Tink, seeing the other woman reaching for her own laser pistol. Wendy couldn't still the impulse and reached for a glass someone had carelessly left on the banister. With precision, she threw in in Tink's direction, smiling with satisfaction when it collided with the Faetian's temple, dropping the little sprite to the floor, where she twitched and groaned heavily. She was still alive, which was good. Wendy didn't want her to die. Probably.

Her attention returned once more to Peter and Hook, who seemed to, by unspoken mutual agreement, face off while the others stood idly by. It seemed like such a male thing to do and was clearly some display of machoism, but that didn't mean it left her unaffected. Seeing Hook wielding a proper sword with such skill and confidence made her heart race and her panties damp.

Peter's looked like a toy in comparison, and though he was a skilled swordfighter, it was obvious he didn't have the stamina or the expertise that Hook had, and he was clearly losing. With a growl of what sounded like impatience, Hook suddenly shoved Peter against the wall, knocked aside his ineffectual laser sword, and pressed the point of the electrified sword close to Peter's throat without touching.

He spoke to Peter in a low tone, and Wendy was too far away to hear what they were talking about, but she grew uneasy when Peter looked at her, and Hook's gaze followed. When his eyes settled on her, including the cybernetic one, she trembled as a shock went through her. She wasn't certain exactly what prompted it, but there were definitely elements of fear and excitement.

Both emotions amplified as he tossed Peter toward his crew, who were quickly rounded up and surrounded by the other four who'd backed up Hook as the man strode toward her. He was poetry in motion, and it left her frozen to the floor like an idiot. Before she could even think about trying to run away, he was already in front of her. He reached for her, and she almost took a step forward to meet him. Only realizing how ridiculous that would be when she knew nothing about him kept her frozen in place.

A moment later, he picked up her arm and started tugging on the bracelet. It was instinct to fight back, both because she didn't know or trust him, and because the bracelet seemed like it meant something, if not to her, certainly to Peter. She resisted as he kept trying to take it off unsuccessfully.

"Captain, we have a message from Cookson. He says *The Bogey* appears to have found us, based on its current trajectory, so we need to clear out."

Wendy didn't know him at all, but she could see frustration and impatience on Hook's face as clearly as if he'd told her that was how he felt. "Thank you, Mr. Smee. Everyone back to the *Jolly Roger*." He turned to look at Wendy for a moment, his gaze appraising. After a second, he lunged forward and lifted her before she could stop him, swinging her over his shoulder and holding her securely despite the way she fought.

"Let go of me. Release me, you brute." She kicked and screamed, glaring at Peter as Hook strode past him without a backward glance. Peter looked almost shamefaced for a moment, but when she called his name, he didn't look at her. He physically turned and looked the other way. "You're a useless, irresponsible, selfish piece of crap, Peter Pan, and I hope I never see you again."

He still didn't look back, and she lost the ability to see him a moment later when Hook swept through the swinging doors, and they closed behind them. She was still struggling, but he seemed to barely notice. He simply stalked up the gangplank of the red and black ship and moved through the corridors like he owned the place—which he clearly did. "Let me go. You can't think to take me with you." She was straining and kicking with all her might, which was only tiring her out while it seemed to expend no effort on his part. "I'll never cooperate with you."

"Settle down." He delivered the admonishment with a single spank across her butt.

Wendy froze in outrage—and perhaps something more—for a moment before renewing her struggles with increased vigor. "Get your filthy, slimy, thieving paws off me, you animal." Abruptly, he dropped her from his shoulder, but arrested her fall to the metal floor so that she landed on her feet with almost perfect grace despite a small misstep.

"Do you kiss your mother with that mouth?" he asked as he put his palm to a biometric panel by the door, and the hydraulic hiss of a door opening sounded behind her.

"My mother's dead, you piece of shit."

His expression didn't change. "We have that in common then, Miss Wendy." He pushed her backward, making her stumble through the doorway, before giving her a mocking bow and closing the door behind him.

She already knew it wouldn't open for her, but she had to try. She placed her palm on the biometric scanner on the side of the doorway, but nothing happened. She was locked in, at least for the moment. Infuriated, Wendy turned to look around the room. It was small and sparse, but definitely masculine. There was some antique sailing décor that appeared incredibly old, like sixteenth or seventeenth-century original Earth stuff. That she remembered that much of Galactic History class was amazing.

Even if the room hadn't born masculine touches in the decorating, it just felt like the man who locked her in here. His presence lingered, as did his scent when she moved around the room, ostensibly searching for a way out, but also blatantly snooping through his things.

There was no way out, save for the door that he had barred her exit from by locking with his palm. There was precious little in the way of anything she could use as a weapon either, but she doubted he had the forethought to plan this room to act as her cell, so maybe there was hope of finding something. He seemed to have snatched her as a spur-of-the-moment decision, which left her perplexed and fearful. What if he planned to ravish her?

As the ship lifted off the ground and

shot into the air, knocking her backward onto his bed, she found the thought far more arousing than she should under the circumstances. Then she looked up and saw something that made her smile. It wasn't much of a weapon, but was better than nothing.

Chapter Two

JAMES RETURNED TO THE BRIDGE TO MEET SMEE AND the others. The vid screen showed Admiral Tikta Croc's Coalition ship's trajectory on the star map. *The Bogey* wasn't yet in visual range. "How long do we have?"

"Minutes," said Cecco, his navigations officer and all-around technical expert. He also doubled as the *Jolly Roger's* engineer. Being Vlorn, there was no question he was tech savvy. His race seemed to have an affinity with all things technologically advanced, so it was a no-brainer to place him in the role of engineer despite his lack of formal education for the position. "I trust you'll plan a course that evades them, Cecco."

"Of course, Captain Hook."

"What if we can't, James?" asked Remy Smee quietly. As James's oldest friend, he'd earned the right to use his first name except in the most formal of settings.

"Are the Twins ready?"

"Aye, sir," said Turley, who must've overheard part of the conversation. "The Twins can be unleashed, but it might be overkill for smashing a Coalition ship, considering their firepower and yield. They can take out twenty square kilometers each, so if you pair them together...well, it's probably more than we need to take out a Coalition cruiser."

"I'd rather have them and not use them than need them and not have them," said James. The pair of TWN prototype bombs had been an unexpected acquisition during one of the last jobs they'd been hired to do. It had required breaking into a testing facility for government weapons, but these had belonged to the Coalition. The irony of how closely that mimicked the situation that had turned him from an honorable Coalition captain to a rogue pirate captain hadn't been lost on him, but credits were credits, and when the client had been willing to pay in a mix of ruthenium and platinum bars that were untraceable, he'd been ready to do what was required.

Being able to pick up a couple of souvenirs in the form of the TWNs had just been a perk. "Let's plan on evasion and tactical maneuvers, since their ship is larger and has more guns than the *Jolly Roger*. But our girl is adaptable and resilient, and she has the best crew in all the galaxies, so I'm not worried." He sounded confident and felt reasonably so. Of course, there was an element of risk when confronting the admiral's Coalition ship, especially in a head-on confrontation, but they'd been evading Croc for years.

"I have a course plotted, Captain," said Cecco. "We can use the dark side of the moon of the fourth planet in a solar system not too far from us to hide our presence. The moon has a high concentration of rhodium, so its reflective properties should bounce Croc's signals back to them. Shall I lay in a course? It means entering ionospace, where they can track us easier, at least temporarily."

James nodded. "Go ahead, Cecco."

"And what of our guest?" asked Smee.

James shrugged. "With any luck, I can get off the bracelet, and she won't be a *guest* for long. Excuse me. I have to go deal with her." For some reason, that idea filled him with more dread than the thought of facing off with Croc's ship.

He felt more than a healthy dose of anticipation as well and didn't bother to deny to himself that he found the petite redhead with the perfect curves far more appealing than he'd like, considering she belonged to Pan. That should be enough to make her unappealing, but it wasn't having that effect. By the time he returned to his quarters and slapped his palm on the biometric panel, he had hidden any revealing tells that might let her know he found her attractive—other than his erection that was at half-mast, which he couldn't do anything to stop.

She was standing in the middle of his room, arms crossed over her chest, glaring at him. She was clearly furious, but there was something adorable about her in that state. He almost grinned until she called him a few filthy names. That wiped the burgeoning smile off his face, and he shook his head. "Such a filthy mouth on such a lovely young woman."

She glared at him. "I grew up in New London, and not in the nice parts. If you want a fucking lady, you kidnapped the wrong bitch."

James moved closer, striving to appear completely unaffected. She was so different from him, having obviously grown up in a different class in far different circumstances than his own illustrious roots, and here they were, standing practically as equals—both affiliated with thieves and scalawags.

At least he knew his crew was honorable to their own code and not a bunch of liars like Pan's. He couldn't say either way whether Pan's girlfriend was likely to be as disreputable as Pan, but he was prepared for that possibility. "I haven't actually kidnapped you. I simply want the bracelet."

She froze for a moment, looking surprised. "You took me just for the bracelet?"

He nodded. "It wouldn't come off, and I need it. Give it to me now, and I'll make sure you're returned to Neverland." He didn't mention that would be via a life pod on the *Jolly Roger*, which would be a rough, uncomfortable, and long journey in such a small vessel that lacked an ionodrive.

She glared. "I'm never going back there."

Her anger seemed to hide a hint of hurt, and he wasn't certain that was provoked by his mention of Neverland, but suspected it had more to do with when he had affirmed he'd simply taken her for the bracelet. She had worn a wounded look since that moment. It disappeared a moment later, and her expression became pure anger again.

"Wherever you'd like then. I'll drop you at the next safe spaceport. But give me the bracelet." He added a hint of steel to his tone with the request, so she understood it was much more along the lines of a command.

"You can't have it."

He let out a long sigh and scowled. "I will have it, Miss Wendy." He strode toward her, jerking her into his arms when she didn't back down. She almost threw herself against him, which could be mistaken for enthusiastic passion if he hadn't seen the pure rage in her eyes.

She lifted a hand to claw his face, and he clamped his fingers around her wrist, pointed it to her side and held her in a way that she couldn't damage him. She was like a little wildcat, and it took considerably more strength than he would've expected to subdue her. She continued to wriggle as he pulled her into his arms, pressing her back against his stomach in an attempt to hold her in a better position for accessing the bracelet.

He lifted her hand and tugged at the bracelet again. She managed to wiggle free her other hand and elbow him in the solar plexus. His breath left him in a rush, and he reeled back as she shot forward. This time, she didn't go for the door, apparently having realized it was locked from the moment he placed his palm on the panel inside.

Instead, she ran for the display he kept mounted to the wall. Inside the glass box, there were antique pieces handed down from an ancestor who'd once served in the British Royal Navy. He winced as she broke the glass with her elbow, both at the shattering sound and her grunt of pain.

She went straight for the dagger, and he didn't slow down as he approached her. If he gave her time to think and plot, he was half-convinced she'd find a way to use the dagger effectively.

Instead, he barreled into her at full force, clapping his hand around her wrist as he drove her backward until he had her pinned to the bed, where they both fell as she lost her footing. She was still trying to stab him, the feisty little minx, and James applied just enough pressure to make her drop the dagger, hoping he tempered it so she wouldn't bruise. He had no desire to leave marks on the young woman.

Or perhaps just a few marks of passion, like the imprint of his teeth in the skin of her neck, or half-moon indentations from his fingerprints pressing into the firm, yet luscious, globes of her ass as he pounded into her.

She continued to thrust against him,

44

trying to get him off her, but she was only perilously close to getting him off. Her body rubbing against his was making him hard, and he couldn't resist thrusting against her lower regions. When she felt the full weight of his cock pressing against her, she froze, her eyes wide. She looked uncertain for a moment, and then she licked her lips. Her eyes widened, and her body softened slightly against his.

All the signs of surrender led him to temporary insanity, and he lowered his head. In that moment, he forgot all about the bracelet or why they were fighting. All he could think of was pressing his firm lips to her soft, full contours and tasting what he was certain would be the honeyed sweetness within. When she wet her lips again, he groaned, and his lips hovered near hers.

He was on the cusp of tasting them when pain like he hadn't known suddenly filled him, originating from his testicles. He groaned and rolled over, cupping himself. She had kneed him firmly in the groin, and he felt every bit of the pain radiating outward. He was so weakened and incapacitated in the moment that he couldn't even keep her from scooping up the dagger. He expected his pain to be compounded by the dagger sliding into his neck or human eye, both of which were easily accessible to her in his vulnerable position.

Instead, she bounced off the bed and ran to the door. He was still in a world of hurt, viewing everything through a red haze, as he watched her plunge the dagger into the electronic control panel over and over until the door shorted out. He expected her to start shaking from the electrical current passing through the knife, but she must've managed to avoid getting electrocuted, because the door opened a moment later, and she disappeared through without hesitation.

It took James considerably longer to get to his feet, and the first few steps were pure agony, but he had shaken off the worst of it by the time he passed through the room's doorway and out to the corridor. He looked around for her, not surprised to find her by the life pod dock on this level of the ship. She was trying to bypass the system, and he was thankful she hadn't tried her dagger trick again, since it was already going to require a time-consuming repair to fix the lock on his door.

He managed to saunter over to her, though each step was still painful, and stand as though his balls weren't on fire. "What are you doing, love?"

"Getting the hell out of here."

James chuckled. "Not with these life pods, you aren't. They only respond to and recognize the biometrics of my crew. You're at my mercy, little girl, and I'm not feeling particularly merciful right now."

She didn't appear at all afraid. She simply blinked at him and then gave him a wicked smile. "But I bet you're feeling a lot of pain in your balls?"

He growled at her, but conversely, he wanted to chuckle. She was infuriating and irritating, but he hadn't had this much fun facing off with an enemy in a long time. "Come with me." He clamped his hand around the wrist with the bracelet, somehow unconcerned about the dagger. She seemed to have no intention of using it on him, and he was barely having to drag her along. It was more like a coaxing tug every now and then as he led her to the bridge.

He walked over to Cecco's station and thrust out her wrist. "Can you take this off, Cecco?"

The Vlorn looked confused for a moment. "What do I know about jewelry, Captain?"

James chuckled. "It's keyed to her DNA as some kind of security feature. Are you able to remove it with or without her cooperation?" He let his voice hold a threat directed strictly toward her, though he had no intention of hurting her. Wendy was an intriguing minx, and he wanted to know more about her even though she Pan's girlfriend.

CHAPTER THREE

SHE WAS AWARE OF THE THREAT IN HIS TONE, BUT didn't feel particularly frightened. Right now, she was simply angry while also disappointed. It was disconcerting to admit to the disappointment, because she couldn't pretend it originated from any other reason than the fact he wasn't interested in ravishing her.

On the other hand, he'd certainly tried to kiss her. She was positive that was what his body language had implied, and she was on the verge of kissing him back. It was only when she realized that thought should terrify her rather than arouse her that she had managed to respond by kneeing him in the groin instead of parting her lips and accepting his with relish.

At the moment, it didn't seem like the wisest use of her resources to resist allowing Cecco to examine the clasp on the bracelet. She stood passively, and as he tugged at it, an idea occurred to her. She tilted her head and looked at Hook. "I'll make you a deal."

He looked from where Cecco was examining the bracelet to her, meeting her gaze. "What kind of deal?" He appeared impassive, but there was a note of interest in his gaze that he couldn't hide. Even his cybernetic eye seemed to reveal his emotions as well as the one brown eye he still had.

"I'll cooperate with whatever you need to get this bracelet off, but I want a ride

HOOKED

back to New London."

"On planet Nexa?" asked the handsome young man standing near Hook.

Wendy recognized the hint of Irish brogue in his accent and nodded. "Yes, and you must have been in New Dublin?"

He nodded, which brightened his features. He was attractive, but she felt no attraction. She seemed to be tuned strictly to Captain Hook when it came to arousal, at least around here. She questioned whether she would still find Peter attractive either, especially after seeing him contrasted against Hook's virility. *Nope.*

"I was born in New Dublin, but my grandfather and grandmother came from the original Dublin on Earth, before it became too overcrowded."

Wendy relaxed slightly at the friendly exchange. It was difficult to keep her adrenaline levels pumped up when they were having such a mundane conversation, and there appeared to be

51

no active threat. "It was the same for me. I was born in New London, though I believe my family came over a few generations before yours. I can't trace back how far, but I know it was after the Marburg virus decimated about thirty percent of the population in London when it mutated to become airborne. I believe that would've been around twenty-one oh four?"

The man shrugged. "Mighta been. I didn't get much schooling."

"My mother was a stickler for it." She shrugged. "Anyway, we Darlings were mostly New Londoners, except my parents worked for the Coalition Terraforming Corporation, so we spent some time on various planets starting the terraforming processes."

Wendy stopped speaking for a moment, overwhelmed as she recalled the moment when she looked out the life pod window in time to see the structures exploding after the Krolilan aliens had destroyed the structures they claimed were illegally built on a planet in their sector and not caring those structures still held living humans. She, her brothers, and their grandmother had been on the last life pod to successfully launch before the destruction.

"That sounds exciting," said the man with the Irish accent. "I never did nothing exciting 'til I met up with James, er, Captain Hook. Then it's been one adventure after another, lemme tell you."

"I'd love to hear about them," said Wendy.

"Enough," said Hook in a hoarse voice that suggested he was irritated.

Wendy peered closer, because he was irritated, but he also appeared to be...jealous? Could he be bothered by her talking to a man on his crew with whom she had something in common, even if it was only the remote connection of having grown up in different colonies on the same planet? Surely not, because that would imply he wanted more than to bed her. Perhaps he didn't even want that, and the almost-kiss had been a distraction he planned to use to pry off the bracelet.

That brought her thoughts full-circle, and she focused a cool gaze on him. "Do we have a deal then, James?" She used his name brazenly, practically daring him to reject permission.

He didn't answer her. Instead, he looked at Cecco. "Do we require her cooperation, Cecco?"

Cecco seemed to think about it for a moment before shrugging a massive shoulder covered by dark-brown skin with rough patches, almost like tree bark. He had to be at least part Vlorn, if not fully. "It probably wouldn't hurt, Captain The only other way I know of getting it off otherwise—and I'm not even sure it would work—is to kill her. I suspect the security device is powered by her own nervous system, and if you interrupt the flow, it should short-circuit the security system. But it's probably pretty sophisticated, and I doubt we can fool it into thinking she's dead, so if she wants to live, I guess we need her cooperation."

"If *I* want her to live," muttered Hook. He sounded ominous as he said the words and glared at her.

Wendy was confident he wouldn't follow through on the threat, though she had no credible reason to be sure of that. From what she knew of him, she should be terrified that he would simply cut her throat, wait for her to bleed out, and take the bracelet then.

"You could just cut off her hand," suggested one of the crewmembers helpfully.

Wendy flinched at that, but surprisingly, so did Hook. He squeezed his right hand, and it seemed to be more than a reflexive action as he shook his head. "Never." He let out a long sigh and rubbed the bridge of his nose as though he was developing a headache.

Finally, he looked at Wendy. "Very well, Miss Wendy, we have an agreement. Your full cooperation to ensure I get the bracelet, and in return, we'll give you safe passage back to New London."

She held out her hand. "Shake on it." There was more of a threat than a suggestion to her tone.

James gave her a wicked grin as he held out his hand, taking hers and holding it for a moment longer than necessary as he shook it. "It's not a problem anyway. We have business near the New London sector."

Wendy struggled to hide her ire that her request wasn't going to put him out too much. She'd wanted to be so damned inconvenient that he never forgot her, long after they'd parted ways.

Realizing that was a strange thought, and it shouldn't matter if he remembered her, she shoved it aside. Instead, she focused on being all business as she asked, "Now what?"

"Stay out of my way until then." Hook's reply was brusque.

Wendy struggled to hide the silly urge to cry, reminding herself she was stronger than that. She had only cried once after her parents' death, and not a tear since then. This pirate wasn't going to be the one to break her.

CHAPTER FOUR

JAMES SPENT THE NEXT FEW HOURS TRYING TO pretend like Wendy Darling didn't exist. He met with limited success, since his thoughts kept straying to her. He was constantly forcing them to veer back to the task at hand, which was evading Croc's ship while making their way to the Juntarian sector, where they were going to rip off a carefully guarded safe owned by a big crime boss of a small planet. Still, he couldn't stop thinking about her, and it was as though his mouth had a mind of its own when he called out to Smee, "Fetch Wendy."

Smee frowned at him. "Why, Captain?"

James didn't like being questioned, but Smee did it in a way that managed to convey his puzzlement without implying any judgment. "I just realized she can help with our task."

"I don't see how," said Smee.

James shrugged. "She can be a distraction. Besides, I don't want her left alone on the *Jolly Roger* while we're all on the planet. There's no telling what damage she might inflict. You know what she did to my door, right?"

"Aye, Captain," said Smee. He appeared to be on the verge of arguing, but closed his mouth with a slight click instead.

"Well, if you know where she is, fetch her."

Smee nodded and disappeared down the corridor as Cecco appeared from another opening onto the bridge. He nodded at James. "Door's fixed, Captain"

"Thank you, Cecco." He wasn't about to let her have a chance to sabotage anything else on the ship, and that was strictly the reason he was taking her along to the surface. That, and she would be useful for the mission. There was no other motive.

She appeared behind Smee a few moments later and had confined her auburn hair into a neat braid. It hung halfway down her back, and he had to stifle the urge to reach out and wrap it around his hand to drag her closer, both to test the silkiness of her locks, and to have her body pressed against his. He cleared his throat and strove for a stern tone. "I need you."

Her eyes widened. "What do you need from me? I thought you wanted me to stay out of your way?"

"I did until I needed you, and now, you have a role to play."

She was scowling, which conversely

made her more appealing by emphasizing her underlying innocence that she tried so hard to hide behind her tough, filthy-mouthed exterior. "How am I supposed to help, and what's in it for me?"

And why was he seeing that sort of thing when he looked at her? He needed to guard himself against this woman. He crossed his arms over his chest and stretched to his full height. "You promised to cooperate."

She shook her head. "With getting off the bracelet."

"You never stipulated that. So, cooperate, or we can leave you behind on this planet after liberating you from a hand to retrieve *my* bracelet. Take your pick, Miss Wendy." She glared at him, and the flush on her cheeks drew his attention to the smattering of freckles there.

She heaved a sigh and shrugged. "Fine, I'll help. What'd you want me to do?"

"Make yourself sexy."

She glared. "I'm not cooperating in that way, Hook."

He sighed, allowing her to see some of his impatience. "Your task will be to divert Flint while we're accessing the area of his residence that we need. It seems to me the easiest way would be to flirt with him, but if you have a better idea, I'm listening."

She shrugged, and a moment later, the black synth-leather jacket she'd worn slipped off her shoulders to land on the floor the bridge. The blue lighting edging it winked out when it was no longer in contact with her body, so it must be powered by her nervous system—just like the bracelet.

James immediately scowled at the Lost Boys logo on her tank top. He didn't like the reminder that she had been with Peter Pan just hours before. He might've snapped at her to take it off if he hadn't gotten distracted by the fact she was reaching behind herself to slip her hands under the hem of the odious tank top. It took him a moment to realize she was undoing the clasp of her bra, and he shouted, "Stop that."

She froze, looking confused for a moment before her cheeks flushed again, this time obviously with anger. "Make up your damned mind, *Hook*. Do you want me to be sexy or not?"

"That's sexy enough. You want to entice him, not show him everything you have."

"Yes, Captain," she snapped in a faux-servile tone, complete with a jaunty little salute.

James rubbed the bridge of his nose again, feeling the headache there increasing in intensity. "Smee, fill her in a little bit on Necto while I prep the ship."

"Are we taking the lander?" asked Cecco.

"Yeah. We can slip in and out easier than if we land the *Jolly Roger*. It also makes it easier to take off if we get caught and chased." James headed from the bridge after that, not waiting to hear Smee instruct Wendy on the facts of Necto Flint.

They didn't know much about him, other than his vicious reputation, and his propensity for violence. He considered himself a big deal, while James considered him King Turd of Crap Mountain, but conceded he could be dangerous. Necto had an armory at his disposal, along with a small army of thugs, which made it a risky endeavor. The platinum bars he was going to collect at the end of the mission made it worth the risk.

Within twenty minutes, the lander was ready, and he sent out a ship-wide alert for all hands to report. He looked at Cecco as the man, who moved with surprising grace despite his size, was about to slip past James into the lander. "Did you secure the autopilot?"

"Of course, Captain. The *Jolly Roger* will be here when we return."

"And the camouflage?"

Cecco nodded. "They won't be able to scan our ship or read it on any of their equipment. A quick scan of our own confirms that. They don't have any

Coalition-grade communications or sensors detectable on the planet."

"Very well." James answered Cecco, but his gaze was drawn to Wendy. She was walking with Smee and about to step onto the lander. He put out a hand to stop her for a moment and jerked his head for Smee to continue onward. He looked at her, trying to sound reasonable when he said, "Watch yourself with Necto Flint. He can be dangerous, and I prefer to get the bracelet off without you having to die."

"I'm touched by your concern," she said with a dose of sass before sashaying onto the lander. James followed behind, trying and failing to resist the lure of looking at the lush curve of her buttocks.

A short time later, he landed on the planet, which had no official designation in the star charts and databanks, but was informally known as Flint after its narcissistic owner. Smee and Cecco had already scouted out a discreet place to park the lander, so they left it there and covered the last few klicks on foot. Soon enough, they approached the huge building that Flint called home. It was more like a fortress, but with Cecco on their side, James was confident they would get inside and through any security features.

Casting a glance at the smaller building several hundred feet away, he was more nervous about that. That was where Necto liked to hole up and gamble for hours, while drinking Juntarian fire whiskey. That was a lethal combination if it riled him enough, according to their intel from his client, Necto's former mistress.

He turned to Wendy, dragging her close for a moment. When she started to struggle, he frowned at her. "Hold still." He reached into his pocket to remove a camera. It was cleverly disguised as a barrette, and he managed to fasten it in her hair in a way that didn't look strange or have someone questioning why she was wearing it with the braid.

She reached up to touch it, and her fingertips moved quite lightly over the small object. "What is it?"

"It's a camera, and I can see everything you see with my eye." He tapped the side of his face that housed the cybernetic eye. "So, don't try anything funny, like warning Flint. You might think you'd be getting help, but he makes us look honorable."

She rolled her eyes and turned to Smee, as though James wasn't worth an answer. "Where do I go from here, Mr. Smee?"

"You may call me Remy, Miss Wendy. And you want that smaller building over there. That's his private saloon, where he does all manner of foul deeds. As the captain says, please watch yourself."

"Thank you, Remy." Those were the last word she spoke as she departed from them with a straight spine and not looking back even once.

James was conversely proud of her regal behavior while being irritated that she hadn't deigned to even speak to him before parting. The woman was messing with his head.

They waited until she was inside, and James had confirmation that she had engaged Necto in conversation, before heading the other direction toward his home. Cecco was in charge of breaching the technology, and James was right behind him. It soon seemed the intel provided by the client was sound, and it didn't appear that the security rounds had changed in the months since Necto cast Baetrille from his life after growing bored with her.

After confirming the route of the security people, he nodded for Cecco to lead them, and they reached the room that housed the safe a short time later without running into even one security guard.

It was here that Cecco had to start stretching himself, because the security was obviously tight, and he appeared to have some trouble hacking it. It took him almost three minutes. During those three minutes, James found his attention straying to Wendy's view rather than eyeing the hallways as he should be for signs of someone about to approach them.

Wendy was sitting beside Necto at his table now, and the man's hand covered Wendy's. He appeared to try to be trying to drag her onto his lap. She was flirting and giggling coyly, but he could tell from the way her muscles strained and the resistance in her posture that she was genuinely fighting to keep from being dragged onto the other man's lap. He had a visual of Necto turning from a slightly pudgy human into a Venus flytrap that slammed down on her and sucked her in before she could escape. A jolt of guilt hit him at the idea, since it was his fault she was engaged with Necto now.

"We're in," said Cecco softly. The others let out muted cheers there were more exhales than words, and James turned his attention from Wendy's camera feed to the room they entered.

It was little more than closet-sized, but housed a serious safe. This would be a testament to Cecco's skills if he could crack it. It was the first piece of technology that James worried might be beyond his engineer.

He let his attention return to Wendy, who looked uncomfortable now that she had been dragged onto Necto's lap. She was still giving every appearance of trying to flirt and looked lighthearted. It was the laugh that gave her away. There was a frantic, fearful edge to it, to which Necto appeared oblivious.

"And it's cracked," said Cecco with a deep laugh of satisfaction. "I almost worked up a sweat on that one, Captain Hook."

"Almost," said James with a small chuckle. "We're looking for a black box with red calligraphy."

"Cuneiform, I believe it is, Captain," said Smee cheerfully.

"It could be, Smee." James shrugged,

not particularly caring what the proper term was. "We need to secure it in the bag provided by the client, and we're not to look inside."

"I wouldn't mind a slight peek," said Turley with a hint of longing.

"Just a wee one," said Smee.

James shook his head, pretending he wasn't as curious as they were. "I have explicit instructions not to open it, and it's not our business what's inside. Call me old-fashioned or superstitious, but when the client warned me away from looking in there, I was happy to comply." It wouldn't be the first or last time they had retrieved or stolen something without ever learning about the contents of the item.

There were audible sighs of disappointment, but Cookson and Cecco lifted out the box a moment later and placed it into the case the ex-mistress had provided. "And it's loaded up," said Cookson, though James could already see that.

"Let's go." As he gave the directive, James was the first to lead them out. He consulted the sensors from his ship that had tapped into the security system in Flint's house, and now filtered images to him. They had a clear shot, and a clean getaway, except for Wendy.

As they returned to where they had begun, tiptoeing out of the house from a different exit, James cast an uncertain look in the direction of the saloon. "It's time to get out of there, Wendy." She jumped, clearly startled to hear his voice, and he realized he hadn't warned her that there was a tiny amplifier built into the camera that should allow only her to hear it, even if someone else was in close proximity. "Extract yourself."

She nodded subtly as she looked into the reflective surface behind Necto, and he saw her set down the drink she'd been nursing.

"I have to leave now, Mr. Flint, but it was certainly interesting meeting you."

"I'd like you to stay."

"I have somewhere to be, but I can stop by again soon." Her tinkling laugh was patently false.

"I recently sent my mistress packing when she wanted a bigger cut than 'er share. You look like you'd be a tasty replacement for Baetrille."

James cursed as Wendy flinched. "I really can't. Excuse me." She was trying to pull away from his hold and stand up.

Necto let out a growl as he pulled her closer. "Where do you think you're going, woman?" He scowled. "You're off to work in the flesh houses, aren't you? That's the only reason we'd have a newcomer around here that's a woman."

Wendy shook her head. "No, that career path doesn't appeal to me. There's nothing wrong with it, but the idea of strangers pawing me..." She trailed off with a shudder. She was clearly sending James a message.

"If you aren't here for the whorehouse, then why are you on this planet?" His eyes had narrowed in suspicion. "I think we'd better have a conversation, so you aren't leaving yet. We're just getting started. Two more rounds," he shouted to the bartender.

"I really should go, but thank you." Wendy was still trying to slide off his lap with limited success, and having even less success freeing herself from the beefy hand clamped around her forearm.

With a curse, James headed toward the saloon.

"Where're you going, Captain?" asked Turley.

"She requires assistance getting away from him."

"You could just leave her there and let Flint do with her what he wants," suggested Alan Herb, who had a steady gun hand and the loosest morals of the crew.

James grunted at him, not liking that idea at all. "Do I need to remind you that she has the map? We need that, because we all know how life-changing it would be to find the stash, don't we, Mr. Herb?"

At the blond's sheepish nod, he sighed and straightened his shoulders. "Now, what's the best way?" As he asked, Wendy's camera caught his attention again. She was frantically struggling to evade a kiss Necto was insistent on pressing upon her. He reacted without thought, striding toward the bar and reaching for his laser pistol. He kept it pointed toward the ground, but it was definitely in plain sight when he pushed inside the door that stuck and resisted his efforts for a moment.

The screech of the hinges announced his presence better than any alarm system, but he didn't let it slow him down. He simply focused on getting to Wendy, and it became a single-minded goal. When he reached her, he jerked her off Necto's lap. "There you are, flirting again. I've just about had it with you."

She blinked for a moment, but seemed to realize where he was going with the words. She tried to jerk away from his hold. "I have to flirt with someone. You never have time for me anymore."

"I'm a busy man, and you can't expect all of my attention."

Wendy's lower lip wobbled. "Not all, but perhaps even a smidgen. It's like you don't even know I'm alive anymore." For a moment, tears formed in her eyes before she blinked them back.

James was convinced her argument was based more on reality than fantasy, and the logical conclusion was Peter Pan had ignored and neglected her. It made him dislike the little green Faetian even more than he had before, and that was saying something, since the creep had double-crossed him and taken his eye.

"This isn't the way to get my attention. All this does is earn my anger. Are you going to come peacefully?" He turned to glare at Necto. "Are you going to say anything when I take her out of here?"

Necto looked vaguely concerned. "Of course not, mate. She didn't mention belonging to anyone else."

"I'm not a possession," said Wendy

with what seemed like genuine outrage. "How dare—"

James acted impulsively, wanting to nip in the bud whatever insults she might hurl at Necto. At the moment, the gangster appeared more bemused than anything, and he seemed to be buying their angry lovers routine. Chances were, he would just let them walk out as they were, unless Wendy said or did something that Necto perceived as an insult or perceived disrespect in front of his men.

He had to keep her mouth closed, so he slammed his over it in a bid to do so. It started out strictly as a way to silence her, but she tasted as good as he'd imagined, and her lips were so soft against his as they conformed to hers that he forgot why he was kissing her. All he could think about was the kiss itself, and how it made him feel.

"Ahem," said Smee from behind him, which was the first time James realized he'd followed.

James vaguely heard him, but was

incapable of responding for the moment as he continued to ravish Wendy's mouth. It was the best kiss of his life.

"Er, Captain, we should go. Things are tense..."

His words brought a return of sanity and an awareness of the danger they still faced. "Yes," said James as he pulled away with from Wendy's luscious lips with a sigh of regret. "We must go."

That was truer than anyone had yet realized, aside from his crew. Once Necto discovered the theft of whatever the item was in the safe, he would surely put together that James had been there the same day and realize his crew had been the one to steal it. That was why he'd planned to stay out of sight and be discreet, until he had the fool idea of dragging Wendy into it, which had necessitated rescuing her.

He might've made a mistake saving her, but he couldn't allow her to remain at the man's mercy. He tried to pretend he was concerned the map might've gotten damaged if she resisted Necto's advances, but he recognized he was lying to himself as the words filtered through his brain.

When it came down to it, pure jealousy had driven him to intercede. He hadn't liked seeing Necto's paws on her, and he'd been willing to risk everything to extract her from his proximity. Yes, Wendy Darling was definitely dangerous to James's equilibrium, common sense, and perhaps his livelihood as well. He had to keep an eye on her, and more importantly, he had to keep his own reactions in check when it came to the tempting woman.

CHAPTER FIVE

WENDY WAS STILL TRYING TO QUELL THE SHAKES WHEN they returned to the *Jolly Roger*. For a moment, she'd been certain Necto would drag her away from the table and into some room where they would be alone, either to interrogate her, ravish her, or both.

She refused to admit that part of the shaking originated from James's kiss rocking her world. He could certainly kiss well; she had to give them credit for that. It was the single best kiss of her life, and she'd held back nothing. For a moment there, she completely forgot why they were kissing, or that it was all part of the charade to get her free of Necto's clutches. Now, she was having a difficult time looking at James without remembering that kiss, or how passionately she had reacted. It was downright embarrassing.

"As soon as we're back on the bridge, lay in a course for the rendezvous point, Mr. Ceeco," said Hook.

"What rendezvous point?" asked Wendy as she followed him and the others back to the bridge. She half-expected him to ignore the question, since she wasn't officially part of the crew. Seeing how she had nearly been forced to make a huge sacrifice because he'd dragged her into the mission, she felt she deserved answers.

Surprisingly, he turned to her and said,

"We were there to extract something the client wants back. Now, we're delivering it to her."

"What is it?" asked Wendy, her gaze going to the bag two men carried between them. She didn't yet know their names.

"We don't know," said Smee with a hint of longing in his tone.

"We're forbidden to look," said one of the men who'd been carrying it.

"Probably for good reason, Cookson," said James in a firm tone, as though signaling that was the end of the discussion.

"I wonder what it is?" asked Wendy, taking a step toward it.

"Don't even think about it," said the captain as he glared at her.

She liked his stern tone more than she should. In response, she felt the urge to defy him and took another step forward.

With a sigh, he reached out and dragged her closer, keeping his wrist locked around her hand and forcing her to stand beside him as the ship entered ionospace. She stuck out her tongue at him. "For a pirate, you sure are a stickler for rules."

"When it comes to a client, you always follow the rules. It was much the same way in the Coalition." His expression turned bitter for a moment. "Or, following orders there can be a disaster." He cleared his throat. "But following rules in this line of work is crucial. There must be a chain-of-command. It comes down to that, so the client is in charge, and we follow his or her wishes."

She nodded, trying to cull her curiosity. "Yes, Captain." She was unable to keep the hint of mocking from her tone, leaving him no doubt the title was one of disrespect.

He just shook his head, as though he'd given up on her, before asking, "Didn't Pan have his own code of ethics?"

Wendy couldn't prevent a sharp laugh from escaping. "I doubt Peter can even spell the word. Not that he's stupid, but he doesn't bother to acquaint himself with things like honesty or ethics. He's an immature braggart, and—" She shut up abruptly, deciding she didn't need to air her views of Peter Pan with a man who clearly hated him. She'd feel awful if she somehow gave Hook an advantage over Peter, wouldn't she? She waited for a twinge of conscience that never came.

"We'll be there shortly," said Cecco.

Wendy was impressed. "I know we're in ionospace, but that's a heck of a short trip."

Ceeco looked at her, and a grin split is normally rough features, though he still had an air of craggy wisdom about him. "I've made some modifications to the ionodrive, Miss Wendy."

She grinned. "Peter would be jealous. It seemed to take forever to get from New London to Neverland."

"Neverland is at the ass crack of Coalition territory," said the one now identified as Cookson. "It took us a while to reach the backwater planet once we figured out where Pan was hiding out. What a primitive place it is too."

Wendy nodded. "Tell me about it, since I was stuck there for months. There's no escape." She shrugged. "But I'm heading home now, as soon as you have your bracelet, so I guess it all worked out."

"What's back in New London for you, Miss Wendy?" asked Smee.

Wendy was aware of James pretending not to listen, but his gaze, particularly his cybernetic eye, seemed constantly cast in her direction, so she was certain he was absorbing every word. That briefly tempted her to invent a waiting lover, but she couldn't explain why she wanted to make him jealous, so she didn't bother.

"My younger brothers and my grandmother. I haven't seen them since I left New London, so it'll be good to be home." At least for a while, until they fell back into their patterns of expecting Wendy to do everything and take charge. She dared hope that her brothers had grown up some in the last eight months she'd been gone, but she figured that was probably a foolish hope.

"We're exiting ionospace now." Ceeco brought the *Jolly Roger* into regular space again, at the edge of the atmosphere of a tiny moon circulating a larger planet.

Wendy's education had consisted of more practical matters after her mother had died, so she didn't know the name of the star system they were entering, but she was certain she'd seen at least the large planet in pictures before.

"Lock on Baetrille's coordinates. She's going to dock with the ship, since neither one of us wants to land here."

"Why not?" asked Wendy.

"It's disputed territory, so there's no telling what kind of security measures are enforced below from the three governments all claiming it's part of their territory."

Wendy frowned at James's explanation. "Why in the world did you pick this place to meet?"

"Because only an idiot goes into

disputed space and restricted zones," said James. "Or someone wanting to avoid observance and detection." A predatory smile crossed his lips for a moment.

"I'm not certain I would've called you an idiot, Captain, but the words didn't come from my mouth, did they? She accompanied the snark with a sweet smile and barely resisted the urge to chuckle when he glared at her.

"A shuttle's approaching, and I've extended our docking coupler." Ceeco pressed a button before turning to look at James. "Should we escort her to the bridge, Captain?"

"There's no need for that. We'll meet her at the docking airlock, so she can be on her way as quickly as possible. Smee, grab that bag."

"Aye, Captain"

Though Wendy wasn't invited, she fell into step behind Smee, who walked a step behind James. He led them with a confident swagger that she'd like to think was all based on bravado, but he backed it up by quiet strength and competency that was unparalleled, at least among the men she knew.

Ceeco must've already initiated the protocol to let the client in, because she stood waiting for them. Wendy's mouth almost dropped open as she eyed the woman's scanty state of dress and curves so ridiculous they made Wendy feel like a boy despite her own lush shape.

"My darling captain," said the woman in a high-pitched voice that was like nails on a chalkboard. She swayed her hips deliberately as she walked toward James, putting a hand on his chest in a gesture that was way too familiar.

James made no move to step back. He simply leaned forward and placed a kiss that seemed aimed for Baetrille's cheek, but landed on her mouth when the woman turned her head at the last moment.

Wendy looked down when she felt pain in her hands, opening her clenched fists when she realized she'd punctured her skin and left half-moon marks behind from squeezing her hands so tightly together. She tried to pretend like she had no idea why she had that reaction and ignore the surge of jealousy compressing her stomach.

"Did you get it, my darling captain?"

"Of course, Baetrille. It's waiting for you in the bag."

She looked down at it and then at Smee. "Would you be a dear and place it on my shuttle for me?" She addressed those words to Smee. Either she hadn't yet seen Wendy, or she was deliberately ignoring her.

"Of course, ma'am."

As he hefted the bag over his shoulder and headed toward the shuttle, Baetrille moved closer to James. There was hardly any distance remaining, and Wendy wasn't confident she could have slid a piece of paper between them. She was glaring about that as she took a step forward, ensuring Baetrille definitely knew she was there.

Baetrille looked at her and frowned before looking back at James. "Who's this, darling captain?"

"Wendy Darling," said Wendy in a saccharine-sweet tone. "I recently joined the crew, if you know what I mean?" She phrased the question coyly, while batting her eyelashes. She strove not to look at James, not wanting to make that implication. After the way they had kissed earlier, he might end up taking her up on the offer he perceived if she pretended to be his lover. She simply wanted Baetrille to stop touching him—though she had no idea why she cared. Of course she didn't care. The woman herself just irritated Wendy. That was all.

"I see." Her lips turned down in a frown. Like the rest of her, they were exaggeratedly plumped and painted a garish orange color. She looked at James through the veil of her lashes with a pouty expression. "I suppose this means you've decided to decline my offer, Captain?"

"With regret, dear Baetrille."

Smee returned then, and Baetrille pressed her body even closer to the captain's, though that shouldn't have been possible. "You could always change your mind."

"I'm afraid not, since we have an agreement," said Wendy briskly as she strode forward. She grabbed hold of Baetrille's arm and half-dragged her toward to her shuttle, literally shoving her through the airlock. "Thank you for your business. Goodbye." She slammed the docking airlock as she finished speaking the words. She waited until an affronted Baetrille stepped into her own airlock before disengaging the system, which worked on a standard basis like every other ship she'd been on. It sealed the smaller shuttle away from the *Jolly Roger* a second later, to her satisfaction.

Then she turned back to face Smee and Hook, who both appeared amused. The reality of how she'd behaved crashed upon her, and she didn't look at either one of them as she strove for a regal stride, with her head held high, and marched straight back to James's room.

Unfortunately, it still wasn't keyed to let her in, so she was forced to stand there until he caught up with her a moment later. He moved behind her, standing close, with his hand hovering over the biometric panel without quite touching it. "What was that all about?" There was more than a hint of amusement in his tone.

"I just didn't care for her. She didn't seem like a very nice person." That was a lame response, but Wendy couldn't do better on the spur-of-the-moment.

"Mmhmm." His hand moved a little lower, but still didn't touch the panel. She was essentially trapped between him and the door. "I'm sure that's all it was."

She stiffened. "You didn't seem to like her either, Captain Hook, or you would've taken her up on her offer." No one had to spell out for her what the offer had been.

James chuckled then and allowed his palm to rest on the panel. The door opened a moment later. "Touché."

Wendy stepped through the doorway and didn't look back, deliberately keeping her gaze averted from him until she heard the door closed behind her a moment later. Then she allowed all the humiliation she felt to fill her. How could she have behaved in such a fashion? It wasn't like she had any stake in protecting the *Jolly Roger* or its crew, other than a ride home.

Or claiming James Hook as her own.

She wanted to squash the voice that whispered *that* in the back of her mind, but couldn't evade the truth. As much she didn't want to, she was attracted to James and hadn't appreciated he was, if not blatantly flirting with Baetrille, at least not discouraging her.

Thinking of flirting reminded her of having to sit on Necto's lap, and she felt dirty suddenly. She went into his bathroom, finding a small shower stall along with a serviceable commode and sink. The setup wasn't elaborate, but would certainly meet her needs.

She stepped out of her clothes and got in the water after locking the door. It was a flimsy lock, since it wasn't keyed to her biometrics, and he could probably easily override it if he chose, but it gave her some semblance of security while she finished bathing quickly and wrapped herself in a towel from the cupboard above the sink.

She left the bathroom and put her dirty clothes on the trunk at the foot of the bed, wishing she'd had a chance to pack anything else. She couldn't bear to put them on again just yet, and she hoped there were laundry facilities on the *Jolly Roger*.

In the meantime, she recalled Hook having several shirts in his closet and decided to liberate one from his collection. She walked over to it, leaving the towel on the bed. As she did so, she realized she was playing with fire. She stood naked in his bedroom, and worse, she was doing it deliberately. Part of her hoped he would burst in and catch her as she was. Her mind insisted on playing out the fantasy of him ravishing her, and she was overcome with longing. She doubted there would be much ravishing involved though, because she was just as likely to be overwhelmed with lust as he was.

The thoughts were making her skin flush and her nipples hard. She turned her attention to the closet and selected one of the loose, billowy white shirts James favored. It seemed to be an older style, and not one she'd seen before, but they looked good on him. They were also soft and comfortable as she slipped on one and inhaled. Despite being clean, it still bore some of his scent and was almost like having his arms around her.

She moved to the bed, but didn't feel at all tired. At the moment, all she felt was horny, and she had no trouble summoning the fantasy of Hook driven mad with lust as he pressed her into the mattress and joined their bodies as one.

As her mind played out the fantasy, her hands slipped over her body, at first caressing her breasts and pulling her nipples before sliding down her stomach. She cupped her mound with one hand while imagining how it would be to have James's face buried between her thighs. Her clit throbbed with need as her fingers parted her pussy lips to glide inside.

She rubbed herself leisurely, but was soon moved to quicken the pace as her fantasy escalated. She imagined it was him there, his tongue inside while her fingers glided around her clit before moving down to press into her opening and pump as she rubbed her clit against the palm of her hand.

It all seemed to last forever, though conversely was only a few minutes, as she submersed herself in the pleasure of fantasy combined with stimulation from her own hand, and soon lost herself in an intense orgasm. Her body shuddered and strained under the force of it, and while it was nice, it wasn't quite satisfying. There was something missing, something that her fingers couldn't mimic closely enough.

She longed to feel his cock inside her, but this tepid release would have to do.

She was lying there recovering from the aftermath when she heard the hydraulic door hiss open. Wendy jumped off the bed like it had suddenly been electrified and turned away from him to look out the port window, as though she hadn't just been lying on his bed. Had he seen her? Had he guessed what she'd been doing?

When she thought she was composed enough, she took a deep breath, squared her shoulders, and turned to face him— while hiding the hand that had recently been in her pussy behind her back. She gave him a nod. "Do you need something, Captain?"

"Access to my room." With those words, along with the flare of his nostrils, followed by a knowing look in her direction, he headed to the bathroom she had recently vacated. At least he made no comment about her wearing his shirt—or touching herself in his bed.

She buried her face in her hands for a

moment, but the lingering scent just reminded her of what she had done, and what he had nearly caught her in the throes of doing. How would that have played out? There would've been a huge amount of embarrassment involved, but she couldn't help thinking it would've led to fulfillment of her fantasies eventually.

That wasn't what she wanted, was it? Did she really want to get involved in another criminal's activities, only to be relegated to the sidelines of his life? What if his crew tried to turn her into their maid/mother? She certainly wasn't going to put up with that again. It was safer to head back to New London and try to quell her thirst for adventure in the more mundane life she could find there. Being with Peter Pan should've taught her that, and she wasn't about to make the same mistake with his nemesis, was she?

She wasn't entirely certain about the answer, especially when he stepped out of the bathroom a moment later. He wore a towel slung low over his hip, but the rest of his body was bared to her. He was muscular and fit, as she'd expected, with more than a few scars.

She was surprised to see the faded barcode on his shoulder that indicated he had once been in the Coalition and remembered his words from earlier. She wanted to ask about it, but couldn't bring herself to do so. She was too busy staring.

As her gaze slid lower, she gasped when she saw his right hand. With his shirt off, she could see the clear line of demarcation where the artificial hand had been joined with his natural skin. Synthetic skin had grown to join with it, but there was a slight variance in color with some striations that were to be expected, as far as she knew, since every person she'd seen with a prosthetic had that same look at the joining location. "What happened to your hand?"

He frowned. "Did your mother teach you any manners?"

"She tried, but she died before they stuck," said Wendy in a sassy way, hoping to cover up her embarrassment from blurting out the question. "You don't have to answer if you don't want to."

He shrugged. "I don't mind. I went after revenge, acting foolishly without forethought, and didn't account for the fact I was severely outnumbered. The person whom I went after planned to chop me up into little bits and feed me to his fish, but my crew rescued me."

That was clearly an abbreviated explanation, but she figured it was all she was going to get out of him from the way his expression was closed. She nodded. "It's a nice hand." What an asinine thing to say.

He arched a brow, looking like he was going to laugh for a moment, but then his expression became neutral. "Thank you. It works just like my other hand, you know? I feel everything with it that I can with the other." As he spoke, he moved closer. "I can feel cold metal, or the heat of the fire. I can also feel the soft, silky, smooth..." As he spoke, he stopped before her, his hand reaching toward her.

Wendy held her breath, wondering if he would touch her. She still wasn't certain how she would react if he did. Part of her wanted to simply melt against him at the first sign of him making a move.

"...freshly washed sheets," he said with a chuckle as he moved on past her to pull back the sheet.

She refused to acknowledge or show her disappointment. "Good for you. What do you think you're doing though?"

"I'm going to bed." He said the words carelessly, dropping his towel just as carelessly as he slid between the sheets.

Wendy did her best to look away, but not before seeing a flash of his taut buttocks, and more than a hint of his large erection. Her cheeks were flushed, and she made a pointed effort to look way above his waist. She was actually looking more at the top of his head as he settled on the bed in a seated position. "Why are you getting in bed here?"

"Because it's my room and my bed?"

She heaved a sigh. "But I'm using the room."

He laughed. "This arrangement was a temporary cell for an impromptu kidnapping. I certainly never agreed to give up my room, Wendy."

She pointed to the trunk and a hardback chair near it. "Why don't you make a bed with those two things?"

James shot them a look full of disbelief before looking down at his body and up at her. "How would I fit on them? They might fit you."

She glared at him. "You're not much of a gentleman, are you?"

He grinned. "When did I ever claimed to be, *Miss* Wendy?"

She heaved a sigh of frustration. "I'm not sleeping on the trunk with the hardback chair. You kidnapped me, so it's your responsibility to give me a comfortable place to sleep."

He shrugged and patted the side of the bed beside him. "There's plenty of room for both of us, love."

She glared at him. "Don't be ridiculous."

James chuckled. "Suit yourself, but don't claim I didn't offer you a comfortable place after kidnapping you."

"Lying beside you would hardly be comfortable, Hook."

His lips quirked, but he didn't respond other than to turn on his side facing away from her.

If she had a dagger, she would've plunged it into his back right then. She almost wished for Peter's ridiculous laser sword for a moment in her blind anger.

In a huff, she tossed back the sheets on her side of the bed and climbed in with him, turning her back to his. She gave him the deliberate silent treatment, but it didn't work when he refused ask her questions or speak. Was he giving her the silent treatment as well? The thought had her stewing in anger, and as she laid there, she grew angrier still that he had invaded the space she considered hers for the time being.

To think she had just been masturbating to thoughts of him—it boggled her mind. What the hell did she possibly see in this infuriating, irritating man?

"Stop thinking so loudly, or you'll keep up the whole ship," said James with a chuckle.

"You're a bas—" She managed to bite down on her tongue to keep the insult from springing from it. She refused to give him the satisfaction of showing how angry she was. He was giving her indifference, so she could see that and up the ante with cold indifference.

Making a conscious effort to close her eyes and breathe until she felt more relaxed, she focused on composing herself and ignoring him. He was right. There was plenty of room in the bed, and she wouldn't give him the satisfaction of leaving it. Or speaking to him again until he spoke first, so she could implement the silent treatment.

1

SHE woke feeling too warm and quickly realized why. It had nothing to do with the bedding and everything to do with being plastered against James Hook. Her front was pressed against his, and her face was nestled in the curve of his shoulder. She jerked back and looked up, making him rouse as well.

They stared at each other for a moment as it seemed to dawn on him as well that they had ended up moving toward each other and cuddling in the middle of the night. She started to pull away, and his arms seemed to tighten reflexively around her for a flash before relaxing. Neither of them spoke, and then the reason why they had both awakened sounded again—klaxon alarms alerting them there was danger.

Hook rolled out of bed, and Wendy barely had a chance to appreciate any of the view before he strode across the room and scooped up his clothes. He moved to the intercom in his room to contact Smee as he finished dressing.

"What's going on?"

"Croc and *The Bogey* are on our tail," said Smee."

"Take evasive action, and I'll be there in a moment."

He didn't even look back before he departed, but Wendy understood the urgency of the situation. He didn't even close the door behind him in his rush. She slipped from bed to gather her dirty clothes, regretting that she hadn't had a chance to wash them. Since the door was open, she went into the bathroom to change before emerging a bit later. She started to lay James's white shirt on his bed, but changed her mind at the last moment and slipped it over her tank top before tying the tails into a knot at her midriff to make it fit better.

Then she left the room and headed for the bridge, getting thrown into the wall more than once as the ship listed around. She made slow progress, but when she reached the bridge, she found controlled chaos. There was an air of fear about everyone, including James, but his was tempered with calm confidence that seemed to suffuse the rest of the crew, including her.

"Evasive maneuvers aren't working, so we have to get creative. On my mark, I want you to enter ionospace, Ceeco."

"Sir, that might not be a good idea. There're several breaches in the ship, including one in the hull of this room. It's only being held closed by the weakening forcefield." Smee was sweating.

"I know, Remy, but what choice do we have? *The Bogey* is twice the size of the *Jolly Roger*, and Croc outguns us. He won't be expecting us to take the risk, so we have to do it. By the time his nav officer compensates, we can hopefully be out of their range or safely in hiding. Find a similar spot to jump to, Ceeco—and try to jump out of ionospace quickly too. We know we're easier to track in ionospace, so ghost us if you can."

"Aye, Captain" Ceeco appeared to study the star charts on his console for a moment before tapping in a course. "Everybody, brace yourselves."

Wendy looked around for something with which to brace herself, unsure where to take shelter and be out of the way. James must have the answer, because he pulled her against him, and they leaned against the wall together. She clung to him as the ship halted and bucked for a moment, jolted from the abrupt drop to no speed that was required before they could enter ionospace. The ship jerked and whined when they entered ionospace a moment later, blasting far away from the ship chasing them.

As they traveled, the ship started to shriek and shake, and it was obvious the *Jolly Roger* was at its limits. She clung even tighter to James, unconcerned about showing her fear that moment. She just wanted him to hold her and tell her everything would be all right, but she could never hear any words of reassurance anyway over the shrieking sound.

"We'll be dropping out again shortly, Captain." Ceeco must've found a planet. James moved toward his console, apparently looking at the star charts, and she didn't let go of him even when he moved to speak into the intercom system. "All hands, evacuate. The *Jolly Roger* might not hold up for reentry to normal space, and your safest bet is in the life pods."

After he finished speaking, Ceeco looked at him. "I'd like to stay with you, Captain"

"I planned to ask you," said James. "I need someone to fix the ship after she crashes."

"And I'll be staying too, Captain," said Smee, phrasing it as a foregone conclusion.

"I wish you wouldn't, Smee. There's no reason for you to take the extra risk when you can still get on a life pod."

"It's a risk to launch a life pod in ionospace too, Captain, so I'll take my chances with you in the *Jolly Roger*."

"Very well, Smee." James turned to her then. "Do you remember how to find the life pods? I'm needed here on the bridge, but I'll take a moment to show you if you need me to?"

Wendy shook her head, giving in to impulse. "I'm not leaving either."

He scowled. "Don't be ridiculous. There's no reason for you to risk yourself by staying on the bridge with us."

"I don't know your men, and I'm not sure I can trust them."

He glowered in his affront. "My men would watch after you."

"I'm staying here with you. Better the devil you know," she said with a hint of nonchalance in her tone, as though she wasn't terrified—and finding the only comfort in the situation in the presence of the pirate captain who'd dragged her into this mess.

He looked like he was going to continue arguing, but Cecco caught his attention.

"We're approaching the planet I found, Captain. I'm concerned about exiting ionospace and entering its atmosphere though."

"You're a skilled navigator, Ceeco, and I know if anyone can see us through safely, it's you." The captain sounded completely confident.

Wendy realize she was still holding onto James's hand, and she almost let go, but couldn't bring herself to do so. She was frightened, and like it or not, gaining strength and comfort from being this close to him.

The ship continued shrieking, but as their speed decreased when they abruptly shifted from ionospace to regular space, the entire ship shook like nothing she'd ever experienced. There was another, higher shrieking sound that amplified, followed by a splitting sound as they entered the atmosphere.

It sounded like metal being crushed, and air suddenly entered the room—air that shouldn't be there if they still had structural integrity. She started to point it out to James, but before she could, a large crack appeared in the wall she was standing near, pulling her out into the air despite her best efforts to grab onto anything. She lost her grip on his hand, so she was shocked when he dived out of the hull to come after her. His hand grabbed hers, and he held on tightly as he pulled her close to him.

She clung to him, hoping he had some sort of parachute device, but didn't see anything. She couldn't hear anything either, but quickly realized that was because she was screaming so loudly. She managed to clamp a hand over her mouth before burying her face in his chest. She didn't want to see what was coming as they hit a line of trees and descended downward.

They were falling through a jungle, and it felt like they had fallen forever, along with smacking every branch on the way down. She was cut and bruised, but figured those wounds were nothing compared to the life-ending stop waiting at the culmination of their fall.

Instead, they plunged into water. She gasped as she sank below the surface before instinct asserted itself, leading her to kick her way upward. The water was far too hot to be comfortable, but it wasn't quite hot enough to boil her skin or kill her by hyperthermia if she got out soon.

She swam as hard as she could until she broke the surface and looked around immediately for the captain. "James? Where are you?" After a moment, when she didn't see him, she took a deep breath and plunged below the waves again. She looked around as well she could in the murky water, but didn't see him.

When her lungs felt like they were going to explode, she forced herself back to the surface. This time when she broke through the waves, she saw James a few feet away from her. He had his hands cupped around his mouth and was calling her name. He looked like he was about to dive below again to look for her, and she quickly called out to him to keep him from doing so.

They swam toward each other as though drawn by magnets, and she treaded water when she reached him. He wrapped his arms around her for a moment, and it was a hug of reassurance and comfort, but also celebration that they were both still alive. For the moment, it was simply those things, and she felt barely a stirring of desire.

As one, they turned away from each other and started swimming to the shore. It was thick with vines and foliage, but those proved to be a helping hand when they dragged themselves up and out of the water. They climbed up the steep embankment slowly, until they reached the top and found a fallen log sheltered by enormous trees and more vines surrounding them. Wendy dropped down upon it, shaking from reaction to the last few minutes.

James sat beside her, pushing the hair off her face and tucking her now-messy braid over her shoulder as his fingers moved down her arms and over her body. "What are you doing?" Her teeth were chattering from shock, certainly not from cold, and she could barely get out the words.

"I'm looking for broken bones."

"Don't you have a scanner?" She looked at his eye, remembering he'd used it to see through her eyes with Necto.

James shook his head. "I didn't have time to grab one or anything else. I just sort of...reacted." He seemed almost puzzled by that. Then he chuckled. "Except the sensor in my eye." He appeared amused by his lapse of memory as he looked her over instead, scanning her with his gaze. "I don't see any signs of internal bleeding or broken bones. You might have some bruising, and you definitely have cuts."

She nodded. "You too. Is there any way I can use your eye scanner to look you over?"

He shook his head. "But there's no need. The sensor in my eye is tuned into nanotech in my body, so it's reporting back to me. I have no obvious injuries either."

"It seems like a miracle, considering we just fell thousands of feet out of a spaceship."

"I'm thankful for that." He looked up and grinned. "And we have food."

She followed his gaze, looking up to see a leafy tree above them. It was large and bushy, providing ample shade—though not much sunlight got through to the forest floor with the canopy of trees above anyway. She saw big fluffy growths on the tree that looked like green cotton balls. "What is it?"

"It's a mallowberry tree, and the fluff is edible. It has some other benefits too, but food is the most important right now. At least we won't starve tonight."

"You think we should stay here?" She thought it was smart to press on, but couldn't deny she was exhausted and emotionally overwrought after plunging through the air and falling into the water.

Her body hurt from the impact as well.

He nodded "Perhaps Smee and Ceeco can find us with the sensors on the *Jolly Roger*, if it wasn't too damaged when it landed." He didn't sound optimistic about that.

She wasn't feeling optimistic either, and her stomach was still churning when he handed her a handful of mallowberry fluff a bit later. Hesitantly, she tried a bite. From its name and fluffy appearance, she expected it to be sweet, but it was rather tart and citrusy. It wasn't delicious by any means, but was sustenance for the night.

As it started to get darker, the heat from the water that had soaked them faded, and the jungle started to cool too. She began to shiver, and James put his arm around her to pull her against him without a word. She supposed she should protest, but she simply wanted to enjoy the comfort he offered, so she laid her head on his shoulder and snuggled closer, savoring their exchange of body heat, and his proximity.

CHAPTER SIX

JAMES WOKE WITH THE FIRST RAYS OF SUNLIGHT streaking across the sky. He could see the faint outline of a second sun behind the first and assumed it would become hot by midday or so. With that in mind, he roused Wendy despite how peaceful she looked lying against him. She felt nice too, and she smelled wonderful.

In spite of everything she'd been

through, she retained a unique scent that was all her own, and it reminded him faintly of the citrus smell of the mallowberry fluff, along with her own musk. He would've assumed the citrusy scent came from the fluff she'd eaten last night, except she had smelled like that from the moment he pulled her into his arms when they were still in the Lost Boys Clubhouse on Neverland. Her scent had haunted and taunted him since, and he allowed himself a moment to fully enjoy it before she started to awaken.

Her eyes opened slowly, and it was clear Wendy wasn't a morning person. She groaned and slammed her lids shut as soon as they fully opened. "It's too bright. Let's sleep longer."

"I don't think we can, since there are two suns. It's going to get hot this afternoon." He gently shook her shoulder when she seemed to give every appearance of curling up closer to him to snooze again.

She looked grumpy when she finally sat

up and opened her eyes, but didn't argue. "What's your plan?"

"We're going to walk in the direction we last saw the *Jolly Roger*. I'm hoping we'll find breaks in the vegetation that will guide us along the way. If not, the men in life pods will requisition another ship to come find us, or Smee and Cecco will find us after they're finished repairing the *Jolly Roger*."

She frowned. "What will we do if the *Jolly Roger* is destroyed?"

"It won't be." He spoke with confidence, not allowing himself to have even the faintest doubt. The *Jolly Roger* was his home, and it had been the first bit of hope he'd experienced after being dishonorably discharged from the Coalition Navy due to Croc's illegal activities. He couldn't abide the thought of the red and black ship being damaged beyond repair. "Cecco can fix anything."

She looked like she might want to argue, but she just sighed instead. "Where can I see to my needs before we start walking?"

"Pick a tree." He grinned and could see from her grimace that she didn't like the idea, but he didn't have a spare restroom lying around. "I'm going to the left, so why don't you go to the right, but don't go too far. Stay within calling range."

With a groan, she got to her feet, and he held her steady for a moment until she looked like she could walk. He was experiencing some soreness of his own after that plunge into the water. Good thing they'd hit feet-first. If they'd landed on their stomachs or backs, they probably would've died from internal injuries.

He went the direction he'd indicated, keeping an eye on her until he could no longer see her. James tended to his morning needs as quickly as possible before returning to the tree where they had spent the night. He allowed himself a moment of indulgence, remembering how it felt to hold her while they slept, but quickly banished the thought when she returned.

He climbed on top of the log and stretched almost on his tiptoes so he could reach a branch of the mallowberry tree, plucking off several handfuls of the fluff to pass to her so they'd have something for breakfast and while walking, in case nothing else edible turned up.

Once he was on the ground, Wendy handed him a handful, which was roughly his half of the fluff. He nodded his thanks and pointed Northwest, which was the last direction he'd seen the *Jolly Roger* heading when they plunged out of the hole in the hull. Well, she had been ripped out, but he'd jumped after her like a fool. He still couldn't explain what had motivated that lack of self-interest, other than pure reaction. He refused to probe any deeper as he started chewing on the fluff. It wasn't any better than it had been the previous evening, but his empty stomach appreciated something.

"I'm so thirsty," said Wendy a few minutes later as she tucked some of the fluff into the pocket of the ragged synth-leather pants she wore. He tried not to notice how formfitting they were, but failed miserably.

"Do you think that water we fell into is potable?"

He shrugged. "It was really hot, and it's already far behind us. I'm hoping we'll find other fresh water that's farther along in the terraforming process."

She looked intrigued. "This planet is in terraforming?"

He nodded. "The sensor in my eye can connect to the Coalition database. According to that, this planet—K02D—is in the third decade, so there's enough oxygen and some plant and animal life. It's not quite ideal standards yet, with the primordial jungle around us, but we aren't going to die from lack of oxygen in the atmosphere or variance in temperature." Unless it got too hot at midday, when both suns were shining overhead, but he didn't think that was going to happen with the shade of the canopy provided by the jungle. They had more risk of dying from dehydration than from sunstroke. He didn't share that cheerful thought with her as they continued walking.

"What will we do if the *Jolly Roger* didn't make it?" She sounded hesitant as she asked the question again.

His shoulders stiffened, and he shook his head. "That won't happen. Would you like to hear how I acquired the *Jolly Roger*?"

She nodded as she started to stumble over a root in front of her. James reached out a hand to steady her, and they shared a long look. He could lose himself in the sparkling blue of her eyes if he let distraction overtake him. He cleared his throat and looked away as he started walking again. Her hand was in his, and he wasn't certain who had reached for whom, but he wasn't about to break the contact.

He told himself it was so they wouldn't get separated, and he could help her over some of the harder terrain, but the truth was, it was reassuring to have her hands folded in his. The hand was delicate and fragile, with long fingers, and seemed to have little strength, but he was certain that was a deceptive appearance. One thing Wendy Darling seemed to have in spades was strength, and maybe she didn't even realize how much she had. He just hoped she didn't have to tax her reserves on the journey ahead of them.

"It was after... It was after something I don't want to talk about, but I was adrift. It was just me, Smee, and Cecco at the time. We were looking for a way to feed ourselves, and things were getting dire. We managed to hitch a ride on a cargo freighter to a backwater planet and met a disreputable scalawag there." His tone was rich with affection. "Barnaby Dolans was the captain of the *Jolly Roger* then. Old Bones took us on, teaching us the trade and making us part of his crew. A crew that's like family, but he was particularly close to me. He said I reminded him of a son he'd lost years earlier. I never did learn if he meant he lost him to death, or to his own actions by not being there for the kid. Either way, Bones regarded me as a son, and since I was no longer in contact with my family, I appreciated the relationship. When he was on his deathbed, reaching that point after a duel gone wrong, he bequeathed the captaincy and the ship to me."

"He was a pirate too?"

James chuckled. "Of course he was. No reputable ship's captain would've taken me on with the bounty on my head."

"What was the bounty for?"

His face tightened as he scowled, and he shook his head. "I don't want to talk about that right now."

She looked like she wanted to press, but she just sighed and went quiet. They walked that way for a while, trudging through the jungle as they made slow progress. James wished he had Turley's sword to help clear the vegetation in their path.

As though Wendy had read his

thoughts, she suddenly giggled. "What I wouldn't give for Peter's ridiculous laser sword right now. We could slice right through these vines."

James couldn't help an answering laugh that turned to a snort. "It was rather ridiculous, wasn't it? It makes sense for Turley to have one, since a ceremonial sword is a big part of Juntarian culture. They're passed from father to son and mother to daughter. But why in the world would Peter Pan pick a sword over a laser pistol?"

"It's probably because he's never grown up, and it makes him feel dangerous or exciting." Wendy sounded sour.

"*You d*on't seem to have a very high opinion of Pan."

"Nope."

The answer was too succinct to provide details, and he wasn't at all abashed about probing for information. "And yet you're his girlfriend?"

"*Was,*" she said emphatically. "I was

actually leaving him when you showed up. I wasted too long on him as it was. It was soon obvious he was never going to grow up or take things seriously, and he took me for granted. I let him though, but there weren't a lot of options once I was stranded on Neverland. The people who came and went on Neverland were usually shady, at best, and I wouldn't have trusted any of them for a ride." She gave him a meaningful look.

"They just had to kidnap you to earn your trust." He winced when she slugged him in the shoulder, hoping she hadn't intended to hit quite that hard. "I do apologize, but the bracelet was too valuable to leave behind." He left it unspoken, but he suspected Wendy was too valuable to leave behind as well. It seemed like kidnapping her might've been one of the best decisions he'd ever made.

1

THEY walked for a couple more hours, but the heat of the day just increased. Even the canopy above them couldn't completely shield them from it, so it was a relief when they came across a stream of water in their path. James spent a moment analyzing the sample with the scanner, doing so by plunging his finger into the cold water so his nanotech could interact with the sensors in his cybernetic eye to analyze the contents.

He could see Wendy's disappointment when he shook his head. "We need to boil it first. There are too many organisms in it to be safe to drink without doing so. We don't know how some of them will react in our bodies, and the others that are present definitely have known issues that we don't want to deal with."

"But I'm so thirsty." She almost whined the words, and then shook her head. "I'm sorry to be complaining. All I can think about is water."

"I'm feeling the same way, so let's get this done, right? Let's build a fire, and we'll purify some water."

They scattered, but stayed within

audible range of each other, as they searched for sticks he could use to build and start a fire. Wendy returned with a couple that looked like they would work, and James had found enough for kindling and the beginnings of a fire. Together, they fetched stones from the stream to build a small firepit. The last thing they needed was a raging forest fire consuming the jungle from which they couldn't escape.

A short time after he started trying, James concluded starting a fire with sticks was harder than it looked, and he couldn't get it to catch. He tried for another five minutes before he was driven to the verge of cursing. "This was in our Coalition survival manual, but I never expected to actually need the skill."

"Let me have a try," said Wendy.

James didn't think she was going to fare any better than him, but he handed over the sticks and moved out of the way so she could give it a shot. He wasn't certain whether to be happy or a bit miffed when she had smoke a couple of moments later that quickly turned to fire. "How did you do that?"

She grinned up at him. "I grew up mostly on New London, but we spent a few years on different planets in various states of terraforming. It allowed my father to teach us all some survival skills. Honestly, I was never able to master this when he was trying to teach me, so I think it's just blind luck that it worked this time."

"Whatever it is, I'm thankful." He looked around. "Now I need something to put water in for the purification."

Once more, they entered search mode, but this time they were focusing on the rocks in the stream along the edge. James found a rock that had a deep enough depression to give them at least a couple of servings of water. It would be slower than he'd like to get enough for both of them to sate their thirst, but it would have to do.

Balancing the rock as carefully as he

could with as much water as it would hold, he moved back to the fire and placed it over the top. He looked up as he did so, noting how high the second sun was in the sky now. They'd be lucky to be able to walk a few more hours, and he doubted they would find the *Jolly Roger* today. He didn't share that with Wendy as he leaned back against a tree and waited for the water in the rock to start boiling.

l

A few hours later, he was sweating heavily, and so was Wendy. The water they had earlier was long gone, since they had no way to store or carry it, and it was too hot to go much farther. "Keep your eyes open for somewhere we can take shelter from the heat of the afternoon, since it's getting so hot out here."

"And for more water," said Wendy. She sounded hoarse.

He was worried about her stamina, but she'd kept up so far, even with being thirsty again. So was he, but there was nothing they could do about it at the moment, since they hadn't run across more water.

They walked for another twenty minutes, pushing through the thick vegetation that seemed particularly stubborn here, before James literally stumbled into a cave. He tripped over a thick vine and plunged forward, landing hard on his hands against rock. It was a few feet above where he should've landed, when he'd expected to hit the ground, and the impact knocked aside bushes that had obscured a good part of the opening. He spent a moment looking closer, discerning the bushes had grown that way, rather than been arranged. If they had been arranged, that meant there was something or someone intelligent on the planet with them, which could either be good or bad. He was relieved to see it was a naturally occurring pattern as he pushed the foliage back and balanced himself on his hands to lift his body into the narrow space.

Fortunately, once he was inside, it segued to a taller opening, and he could almost stand upright. It was small and cozy, with a faint musty odor that suggested something had lived there in the past, but it didn't appear to be an active den belonging to any creature at the moment, and he deemed it suitable if they could find water nearby.

He wiggled out again, surprised to feel Wendy's hands cupping his buttocks as he did so. They were gone a moment later. When he was on his feet and could see her, she looked vaguely embarrassed. He arched a brow.

"I was trying to help steady you. You came out faster than expected." Her cheeks were flushed, once more emphasizing the freckles there, and he found himself counting them. Seventeen. And one right on the tip of her nose, which made eighteen. It was an adorable, if useless fact, that he tucked away in his brain for reasons he couldn't explain.

"I think it'll do for the night, at least. That's assuming we can find food and hopefully some water nearby.

She looked exhausted, and there was relief in her eyes. "I hope we can find water."

James pulled her closer, and her eyes widened. She licked her lips, and he was certain it was an invitation to kiss her, even if it might not have been consciously given. With regret, he ignored the invitation and used the small knife he kept in a scabbard on his ankle to cut a piece of fabric off his shirt that she wore. She gasped as he held up the white material. "I'm going to tie this on the branch near the cave, so we can find it again."

"Can't your sensor just mark the coordinates?"

He shrugged. "It's kind of hard orient myself with latitude and longitude when I don't know what it is for this planet, or what location we're at. Other than a compass that seems to be accurate, I'm about as blind as you are, no pun unintended." He winked at her with his cybernetic eye, which elicited a faint smile.

"I guess we should look for food and water."

He nodded, having her stick close. He was no longer holding her hand and keenly missed the connection, but tried to pretend like it didn't matter. Wendy was nearby, and he could feel her presence even if they weren't touching. That was enough to reassure him she was okay and alive, and so far, they were safe.

They ended up covering about four kilometers around the radius of the cave before discovering a trickle of water bursting through the rockface. He couldn't help a laugh of delight when he scanned it. "This is safe enough to drink as is. Probably because it passes through enough obstacles and minerals to purify it."

Wendy issued a cheerful sound of her own as she cupped her hands under the trickle to catch water that she gulped from her palms. James did the same. They drank their fill, and then he couldn't look away as she wetted her hands again and dribbled it over her hot face, slowly cooling down so that the red flush dissipated. He did the same, particularly on his neck under his beard, which was itching like crazy. He made a mental note to shave as soon as he had time once they were back in the *Jolly Roger*.

"I wish we could take some with us." She looked around before eyeing a plant with large leaves. "Can your sensor tell you if it's safe to eat that plant?"

He shrugged. "Only if something is in the database. Does it look edible to you?" Perhaps she had seen something similar on the terraformed planets she'd resided on as a child.

"I'm not sure, but I think we might be able to fold the leaves enough to make a bowl to take a little bit of water back with us and not have to make the walk back here until morning."

He reached up to pluck one of the large leaves off the tree and held it in front of his eye. It was larger than his head, and he could see from the shape of it that it should be possible to bend it to hold water. A quick scan revealed no known toxins in the plant, which didn't quite make it safe, but made it likely that it was *possibly* safe.

He shared that information with Wendy, and she nodded. "I think we should risk it."

"I agree, but let's see if it's reactive to our skin first." He took the leaf and crumpled it so the side that would hold the water was facing outward before rubbing it across his forearm. He waited for burning or a stinging sensation, but nothing happened. It could take hours for a reaction to occur, but he was too impatient to get out of the heat to wait here, or come back later. "Let's take the water back in the leaves, but we can't drink it until we wait to see if a rash develops."

She sighed before reaching for another couple of handfuls of water. "I think I can live without water for a while."

Between the two of them, they managed to fashion shallow bowls out of a few leaves, and they both carried one back to the cave. Only about half of what they originally took survived the trip, but it would be enough to see them through the night if the leaves they used to carry it proved safe and didn't leak toxic phytochemicals into the water while it was sitting.

Once they had the leaves secured in the cave, he said, "We should look for some kind of food now. I haven't seen any mallowberry trees for a while."

She shuddered. "I'm almost relieved about that. I know it's food, but I don't think I can handle another round of that stuff."

Sharing a grin of agreement, he closed his human eye so he could more easily focus the scanner in his cybernetic eye. It had a farther range than his human eye, of course, and he was able to detect something that looked like fruit and berries in roughly the same direction. Once more, they set out walking, and he was pleased that Wendy didn't seem on the verge of whining about the arduous task. She was a trooper, and she was a helpmate. He had a feeling Wendy Darling was a keeper, but she was probably too good for the likes of him.

They reached the bushes, and the berries proved to be unknown to his databanks, so they decided to pass on them. "Too bad," said Wendy with a sigh as she eyed the fat orange berries. "They look delicious."

"But they could be deadly. Let's see what the fruit is."

They reached that tree a few hundred yards later, though the fruit was out of reach. "Can I give you a boost, and you can grab a few?" At Wendy's nod, he knelt down and wrapped his hands around her thighs, lifting her as high as he could. She barely weighed anything, but he was finding it hard to hold her—simply because his thumbs were so close to the crease between her legs, and he was certain it was growing damper by the moment. He was tempted to abandon the search for food and sate himself with Wendy instead, but his stomach rumbled then, reminding him of how impractical an idea that was. Food now, and Wendy later. His stomach grumbled again, but he couldn't tell which thought motivated the reaction.

Wendy grabbed a few of the oddly shaped fruits. They were somewhere between oblong and rectangular, with rosy skin and what looked like barbs, though they weren't sharp.

Using his knife, James cut one open and touched it with his finger. There was no burning sensation, and the sensor in his eye searched for a moment before finding a match on another terraformed planet in the same sector. It was deemed edible, and he breathed a sigh of relief. "We can eat it."

"I wonder what it tastes like?" She took half the fruit he held out to her, eyeing the peachy interior with its large green seeds. "Is it ripe?"

He shrugged. "I can't tell you that. Let's see what it tastes like." Since it had firm flesh, it required his knife to slice off a piece, and he chewed slowly, analyzing the taste. It was probably a little underripe, but it didn't seem too bad. The flavor was somewhere between plum and liver, and he grimaced.

Wendy popped in a piece, and she groaned. "Everything on this planet tastes disgusting."

"At least it's food." With those pragmatic words, he forced himself to eat his half of the fruit. They had three others remaining, and he looked at the tree. "Do you want to get more?"

She shook her head. "I think three will be enough for now."

He thought about arguing, since they

would still be moving when it was first light, and he didn't want to have to make too many stops for food or water when their travel time was limited to a few hours each day, but he couldn't disagree. It would be hard enough to choke down another piece of the fruit, and he was certain only desperation would drive him back for more.

With that in mind, they returned to the cave, scavenging some more of the leaves and foliage to fashion makeshift beds on the hard stone floor. With the moss and leaves, it wasn't exactly comfortable, but was certainly better than lying on the cool stone.

Wendy was lying near him, but not quite touching. For a moment, he wanted to roll over and pull her into his arms, remembering how it felt to hold her the previous night, but he forced himself to stifle the urge. There was obviously an attraction and awareness between them, but nothing was determined, and no one had declared any intentions. They were still virtually strangers, and he wasn't certain she would welcome his arms around her. He suspected if she wanted him, she would roll into his embrace as she had done on the *Jolly Roger* the night before.

1

A strange howling sound woke him sometime later, and he looked over to see Wendy's fearful eyes. There was a small fire burning, so she must have been up for a while. He nodded to it. "Thanks."

She nodded as that creature held again. A tremble shook her slight frame. "What is that?"

James tried running the sound through the sensors connected to the database, but found no match. It was unnerving, but he just shrugged and tried to appear unconcerned. "It's not too likely to venture in here with the fire."

She bit her lip, looking like she wanted to believe him, and slowly relaxed. "Do you have a rash?" She licked her dry lips, which were starting to crack.

James pulled back the sleeve of his shirt to examine the spot where he'd rubbed the leaf, and it looked un-blotched. "No reaction, so it should be safe enough to drink the water." Just to be certain, he put his finger in the leaf bowl of water, once more scanning it to ensure it hadn't absorbed any sort of contaminants or toxins from the leaves during its time sitting in them. His sensor declared the water safe, and he nodded at her as he reached for one of the leaf bowls.

He sipped carefully, but she was less conservative. He didn't want to lecture her about rationing unless it became necessary. It was getting too dark—a simple glance out the cave told him that—to fetch more tonight, but she was unlikely to suffer too much from the effects of dehydration if she had to wait until morning to get more water.

And he would share with her if she needed it. That inclination toward altruism was a bit unusual for James. He was used to sharing with his crew and looking after them, as a good captain must do, but he'd made a conscious effort to shed all that nonsense about honor, loyalty, and service when he'd been criminally discharged from the Coalition Navy and received a bounty on his head just for following orders.

Of course, Wendy was different. She was a woman. It wasn't that he felt like he needed to protect her because she was woman. More so, it was because of the woman she was that he wanted to protect and shelter her. He'd never experienced anything like it. He was certain she was dangerous when it came to his heart, but he was almost as certain that it was already far too late to stop falling for Wendy.

She looked up then and caught his gaze, and her cheeks flushed. "Why are you looking at me like that?"

"Like what?" He took another sip of water before returning the leaf bowl to the ground.

She put down hers as well and was fiddling with it, as though attempting to evade his gaze. "Like you want to eat me. If you're hungry, there's some of that dreadful fruit."

He laughed softly. "I'm hungry, but not for fruit. I do want you, Wendy." Maybe blunt honesty wasn't the best approach, but he believed in being direct.

"I know," she admitted. Her gaze went to the ground for a moment as she whispered, "I want you too."

At that moment, the animal howled again. James wasn't sure how much was actual fear of the animal, and how much was simply an excuse she seized, but either way, she scrambled across the floor and was in his arms a moment later.

He held her as she trembled for a bit, growing harder at her proximity, but not wanting to rush her. Her heart was pounding as he could tell when he pressed his thumb to her wrist and felt her pulse racing, but he liked to think at least part of that was from being so close to him.

She turned slightly in his arms, lifting her head to his. When her lips parted, it was obviously an unspoken invitation that he eagerly accepted. He molded his to the soft contours of hers, finding her just as tasty as she'd been at the last kiss. This time, there was no audience and nothing preventing them from fully enjoying each other. He didn't bother to hold back as he kissed her with all the pent-up passion that he'd felt since the moment he'd laid eyes on her. She was kissing back just as enthusiastically as she tugged at the buttons of his shirt.

Since he had nothing else to wear, he carefully pulled her hands away and unbuttoned the shirt himself, but somehow managed to do so without breaking the kiss. Then her hands were roaming over his chest, and he was envious that she had that much access when he had little. With the same cool composure he'd shown just moments before, he stripped his shirt off her, but the sight of the Lost Boys logo on her tank top still irritated him. He pulled it off as quickly as he could and tossed it aside without looking.

She hadn't taken time to put on a bra, likely because the ship had been under attack, and she'd deemed it unimportant. He was grateful for that as he cupped her small breasts in his hands. They were perfect handfuls, and her nipples were responsive when he rubbed his thumbs across them. That made her moan and arch her back, and he tilted her back slightly to adjust the angle, so his mouth could settle over one taut bud to suck.

She whined and wiggled against him as he alternated the pressure between soft and firm before gently tonguing the contours of her nipple and dragging his tongue across her chest to the other breast. He repeated the gentle torture there, until she was writhing against him while making incoherent sounds of pleasure. He couldn't understand what she was saying, but she was definitely telling him she wanted more.

He laid her back on the makeshift pallet on her side so he could peel off her synth-leather pants, which proved to be a challenge. He understood the practicality of them in space, since they were resilient. The pants were formfitting, rugged, and also incredibly difficult to remove when she was so aroused. He wanted to cut them off, but forced himself to remain practical, since she'd have nothing to wear tomorrow if he cut her pants tonight.

Finally, he eased them off the rest of the way, then stripped off her panties.

"James, I…" She moaned again as she parted her thighs and lifted her hips. The position exposed her plump lips and pink folds. His mouth watered at the sight of her clit, and he bent his head to taste her glistening flesh. She was sweet and tangy and made the most exquisite sounds when his tongue glided up her slit. They turned to frantic, breathy moans when he started sucking lightly on her clit while curving two of his fingers together to slowly penetrate her.

She was wet and ready for him, and his cock throbbed in response. He stroked her g-spot as he thrust his fingers in and out of her while sucking her clit. Part of him wanted the experience to last for hours, bringing her to the brink before pulling her back to repeat it all again, over and over, but he was too urgent in his need for her to do that.

Instead, he gave her a quick orgasm to take off the edge, and she reached out to grab handfuls of his long hair, anchoring him against her for a moment while her slit quivered, and her thighs tightened around his head. She was calling his name, and it was a beautiful sound with all the passionate release in her voice.

Slowly, her hands loosened enough for him to lift his head, and he discreetly wiped his face before sliding down his pants. They weren't synth-leather, so they were much more agreeable. Even in his haste, they posed little barrier between him and being inside her.

Moments later, he parted her thighs and pressed the head of his cock against her opening, looking down at her. Her eyes were open, and she clutched his fingers with her hands as he held her thighs splayed open. "You have a biochip?"

She nodded.

He'd assumed she would, since it was standard to implant one early in life, but he wanted to be sure. The idea of seeing Wendy swollen with his child was surprisingly erotic, especially considering he'd never really thought about being a father after he became marked by Croc and wanted by the Coalition, but it was definitely the wrong time to indulge the thought.

With a groan, he slid inside her and forgot all about practicalities. The last of his control shattered as her tight walls clung to him, and her thighs wrapped around his waist to draw him in deeper.

He placed his hands on either side of her head for leverage as his lower body pistoned in and out of hers. She thrust against him eagerly, and he felt her sheath tightening around him a few moments later. He almost surrendered to his own orgasm then, but wanted to feel that rhythmic squeezing again. He also wanted to see that same expression of bliss on her face, since it was almost addictive. He moved one of his hands between their bodies so he could stroke her clit, bringing her to the edge of another orgasm.

"I can't, I just can't." She was almost sobbing, yet despite her protests, her hips still thrusted rapidly against his, and now she was rotating them as well to provide extra stimulation with his thumb against her clit.

He was unsurprised when she came a moment later, once more drenching him with her sweet liquid. That time, he could no longer hold back, and his own orgasm burst forth. He clung tightly to her as he pressed his body deeply inside her, keeping them joined together until the last tremors of bliss had faded.

When he was capable of doing so, he turned over to pull her into his arms, holding her against him. Their bodies remained fused, and she didn't pull away. Neither did he. He couldn't find the strength to do so, since being inside Wendy felt like he was enveloped by heaven.

CHAPTER SEVEN

WENDY LAID AGAINST JAMES AND LET SLEEP CLAIM her gradually. A tiny voice was telling her this was a mistake and reminding her she didn't want to end up involved with another space pirate, but she ignored that voice in favor of snuggling against him to soak in his body heat and the pleasure of his semi-flaccid shaft still inside her. Sex with him was even more amazing than kissing and something she wanted over and over again versus her previous limited experiences, which had been over before she'd really begun.

She slept deeply for a while, until that strange howl woke her again. It was closer this time, and she froze before shaking James's shoulder. He quickly opened his eyes as there was a rustling sound at the mouth of the cave. The fire was mostly cinder now, so it provided only a little illumination—but was enough to show the thing was probably sixty pounds of what appeared to be sharp teeth and muscle. She couldn't help a small whimper.

"Stay behind me," said James as he drew his knife. It seemed as ridiculous as Peter's laser sword in the current situation.

They stood up, and Wendy was able to be fully erect, but James had to slouch a bit. She stayed at his side as the creature hissed at them while slipping into the cave. "Did we invade its home?" Her voice sounded frantic to her own ears.

"I don't think so. It might've just smelled us."

She knew what that implied—they smelled like dinner. She bit hard on her tongue to keep in a bleat of terror and firmed her spine as she reached for a branch from the pallet she'd fastened as her sleeping space earlier. It wasn't much, but seemed better than facing it with her bare hands.

It leaped suddenly, and she lifted the branch to swat at it as James slashed with his knife. It howled again, but it was a different pitch this time and suggested pain. She couldn't see the details well enough to be sure, but a splash of something liquid when it jumped hitting her arm made her think it was bleeding, even if the "blood" was a pale green color that reminded her of Tink's complexion.

It jumped at her, and she gasped when James leaped between her and the animal, slashing it again. She was startled and off-balance, so when she tripped, she knocked him into the creature, which swiped a deep gash in his shoulder. James let out a painful howl of his own, but didn't falter. He kept slashing at it until it backed away, and Wendy lunged at it after lighting her branch with the remains of the fire. It howled before leaving the cave. She couldn't look away from the entrance for several minutes, until she was sure it had departed.

When she turned back to James, he looked pale, and he glared at her. She moved closer, though he flinched away. "Can I help?"

"You helped enough when you deliberately pushed me into its path. I guess you do want to be alone." He turned his back on her, but he radiated cold anger.

Her mouth dropped open to defend herself, but she was too furious to speak coherently. She barely restrained the urge to curse at him or call him a rude name. Instead, she turned away from him, determined not to look in his direction.

When she heard him grunting, she

sneaked a small peek, which was enough to tell her he was trying to dab at the bloody wound with a sleeve he must have cut off his white shirt. For a moment, she was moved to offer help by how ineffectual his motions were, but when she considered going to help him, his accusation resonated in her head, and she remained where she was, eventually falling into a restless sleep, where she dreamed about the creature rending her flesh from her bones while Hook laughed and told her she'd brought it on herself.

I

*B*Y morning, she could no longer ignore him. He was moaning and thrashing, and she felt bad for not interceding sooner. She approached hesitantly, standing near his pallet. "Can I help you, Hook?"

He moaned and thrashed again. He sounded incoherent, and his face was blotched and sweaty.

Tentatively, she moved closer, and as she did so, heat radiated off him in waves.

She winced when she touched his shoulder, finding his skin burning up, and the wound looked like it was festering. She cursed again as she reached for the water, only to discover both bowls were empty. She bit her lip before deciding. "I'm going for supplies. Stay here, Hoo...James." It seemed wrong to distance herself from him at the moment, when he appeared to be on the verge of...something she didn't want to contemplate.

She scooped up the leaf bowls and left the cave, at first moving cautiously as she searched for signs of the creature. It didn't appear to be nearby, so she increased her pace as she neared the rockface. After quenching her thirst, she filled the bowls, grabbed several of the leaves, and returned to the cave at a slower pace to avoid spilling the water. She still lost some, but had enough to clean his wound when she returned.

The leaves helped somewhat, but she needed a cloth. Using his knife, she cut a

160

section off the bottom of the shirt she'd stolen from him, which was already missing the tail he'd cut off yesterday. She used that to clean the wound and another section from his remaining shirt sleeve to bind the wound.

Then she bathed his forehead with the tepid water for what felt like hours. When his eyes opened with some level of clarity a while later, she was relieved. "Do you know where you are?"

"Mallowberry," he choked out.

She frowned. "I don't think you should eat right now."

"Fluff...wound." He gestured feebly with his uninjured arm.

With a dubious look, she removed the handful of fluff she'd stashed in her pants yesterday. "You want me to put this on the wound?"

He nodded once. "Fluff will absorb moisture and has antibacterial properties. Bark has pain relief." The words were slurred, but discernable.

Carefully, Wendy moved aside the

bandage she'd just applied to pack in the fluff. It still seemed questionable to her, but he appeared to know what he was talking about—unless the substance that had made him ill was now causing hallucinations. At least putting the fluff on made her feel like she was doing something proactive, so she did it.

He fell asleep again a bit later, and he was still thrashing and moaning. He was obviously in pain, and she recalled his words about the mallowberry bark. She knew it had been at least an hour of walking since they'd seen one yesterday, and she was nervous to venture into the jungle alone. As he continued groaning, and his fever increased, she accepted she had little choice if she wanted to do everything she could so he didn't die. In spite of his unfounded accusation and her anger at him, she didn't want him to perish.

"I'm going to get some bark. Stay here and don't wander," she whispered to him a bit later, though he seemed beyond hearing. She took the knife lying near him, though it didn't feel like much of a weapon when contrasted with the creature that had attacked them earlier.

Wendy headed out into the jungle after finding a sturdy branch to use in case the creature returned, which seemed like a better bet than the knife—which required getting too close to use. She only hoped it didn't come back while James was alone and insensate.

With that thought spurring her, and the vegetation previously trampled from yesterday's incursion, she was able to make good time and found a mallowberry tree about forty minutes after she'd set out. She used James's knife to chisel at the bark until she could slip the blade under it to pry off a big section. Having no idea what part she needed, or how much, she took as large a chunk as she could carry.

It slowed her down a bit, but the jungle allowed her to move faster than she had, due to being on a slight decline and having a rough path cleared now. She reached the cave again thirty-two minutes later and sat beside him. She hated to wake him, but needed help with the bark. "I have the bark, but what do I do with it?"

He groaned, and his lashes fluttered. When he first opened his eyes, they were out-of-focus, and he looked confused. Wendy put a hand on his cheek and stroked lightly as she repeated her question. He blinked and seemed sharper when he said, "Scrape off the soft flesh on the inside and brew it in hot water until it's strong and thick."

She had to leave the cave again to find a suitable rock for boiling water, since the leaf bowls would probably burn up before the water could boil. It took nearly two hours to prepare the tea, but at least he was holding steady rather than worsening.

James tried to refuse the first few mouthfuls, and she couldn't blame him. It smelled a bit like citrus, but earthier, and the tea looked like brown sludge. She couldn't have choked it down, but she was relentless in forcing him to consume some. Gradually, his fever broke, and the thrashing eased. When she looked at the wound a while later, as he slept more peacefully, it appeared less angry and swollen as well. Finally, exhaustion caught up with her, and she dared to sleep, but had the sturdy branch nearby and kept the fire built up much higher this time.

1

JAMES seemed a lot better the next morning and insisted he was well enough to walk a while. Wendy was still angry with him, especially now that the crisis had passed, and she could stew in it, so she didn't argue or try to insist he rest another day. She wanted to find the *Jolly Roger* and get away from James too much to suggest a delay if he was truly up for travelling.

As they walked, Wendy made no effort to speak to James, and he wasn't talking either. She sneaked occasional glances at him to ensure he wasn't taxing himself too much, and though he looked pale, he seemed to be holding steady. He wasn't yet improving, but he wasn't declining either. That was probably the best she could hope for at the moment, and she didn't want to lose him—because she needed him to find the *Jolly Roger*. That was the only reason it mattered.

They'd been walking for a couple of hours when rustling in the underbrush made her freeze. "Is it one of those things again?" Those were the first words she'd spoken to him since that morning, when he announced his intentions to keep traveling.

"I don't think so. It's smaller, I think, but I'll see." He extracted his knife from its scabbard and stood up straight as he moved purposefully toward the area where they heard the rustling.

Wendy thought he was nuts to go investigating, but whatever was making the noise was directly in their path, so if he didn't confront it, they would have to wait for it to go away or try to scare it away.

James let out a sound of satisfaction and lifted his knife a moment later. "Lunch!" Something the size of a rabbit, but completely hairless, was at the end of his knife.

She winced and looked away as he wrapped it in some of the leaves that were now familiar to them and carried it in one hand. When he resumed walking, she followed a moment later.

Wendy walked with him a bit farther, wanting to know why he hadn't stopped to prepare the animal, but determined not to speak to him. She had to live with her curiosity as they continued walking for quite a bit longer, until the sun was scorching overhead, and James stopped in an area that was semi-cleared.

"This looks like a good place to stop and rest." He kicked aside some vines to reveal a bare spot on the ground and nodded toward it. "Would you build us a fire, Wendy?"

Without speaking, she took the sticks she'd brought with her when they left the cave, since she hadn't wanted to have to find a new pair that worked at their next stop. She was having little luck getting the fire started this day, perhaps because of the way he was standing over her, staring. It was intimidating, and she allowed her anger to come to the forefront as she snapped at him, "Stop looming over me."

He frowned, looking confused for a moment before taking a step back. "I wasn't trying to loom. I'm simply waiting for you to get the fire started."

"And judging that I can't get it done. I guess I'm doing that on purpose too." She muttered the words, but not as silently as she'd planned.

He was frowning fully now. "What're you talking about? Are you angry with me? I thought you were just tired and focused on walking, but have you been ignoring me?"

She rolled her eyes as she looked up at

him. "Don't pretend like you don't know."

"Know what?"

"Why I'm angry with you." She tossed down the sticks in a huff, needing a break from the task and from him. She stood up and turned away, taking a few steps that he matched. She turned back to face him. "Can't you just leave me alone for a while?"

"Tell me why you're angry, and what's with the silent treatment."

She crossed her arms over her chest and glared at him. "I'm angry because you accused me of pushing you in front of whatever that creature was. I didn't do that on purpose, and I don't want to be alone." Her voice cracked on the last word, so she looked away from him.

Wendy distracted herself by taking off his shirt that she'd co-opted, since it was suddenly hotter than it had been— perhaps because she was standing in a patch of sunlight that had managed to filter through the canopy. Or more likely because she was embarrassed to have revealed that much about her emotions. She hated coming across as weak or desperate.

"I don't remember saying anything of the sort." He held up his hands in a gesture of surrender when she opened her mouth to protest. "I'm not denying I said it, but I'm trying to explain. Whatever that creature was, it had some kind of venom that started acting almost immediately on my central nervous system. I wasn't in control of myself or my thoughts. Fully rational today, I don't believe you pushed me against the creature. I apologize for saying such a thing and upsetting you."

His words made sense, except he had made the accusation so quickly. "Just how fast did the venom start working?"

He shrugged. "A matter of seconds? I felt off almost as soon as the claws punctured my skin. It wasn't until after you gave me the mallowberry tea and the fever broke that I started to feel like myself again." He frowned. "Did I say anything else?"

She shrugged a shoulder. "You implied that I wanted to get rid of you, so I could be alone. That was it."

He grinned, looking supremely confident. "That's proof that I was out of my mind, since it's clear you don't want to get rid of me."

Something in his confidence stung, and she scowled. "How do you know that?"

"Because you want my body. Sex with me is amazing, and you know it. There's no way you'd try to get rid of me after making that discovery."

"You're such an arrogant..." She trailed off and tossed her hands in the air, once more turning away from him to start walking. She had an inkling that she was going the wrong direction, but didn't care at the moment. She just wanted to put distance between them.

Unfortunately, he wasn't prepared to allow that apparently, because he caught up with her a moment later and spun her around to face him. "Why are you so angry about that?"

"I don't appreciate your overconfidence. What we had—what we did... That was a mistake. We shouldn't ever do it again."

James frowned. "It didn't feel like a mistake, did it?"

She put her hands on her hips. "Maybe it didn't feel like a mistake, but it was. I don't want to get involved with another immature thief."

He blinked. "I'll concede thief without objection, but what makes you think I'm immature?"

She shrugged. "You're being a braggart about the sex thing."

He laughed, and it was a deep belly chuckle. "I'm not bragging. What I stated is fact. That was the best sex of my life, Wendy Darling, and I'll bet yours too. I don't know why you're going to such lengths to deny that when we're already lovers."

"It's just that we shouldn't be." She started to turn away again, but his hand tightened on her shoulder as he pushed her against a tree. She glared up at him. "How dare you?"

"I dare, because you need a reminder of just how good it was between us." With those words, his mouth pressed against hers. It was a hungry and intense kiss, while also full of anger and longing. Wendy alternated between the urge to stroke his tongue with hers or bite him when it surged inside her mouth. For a moment, their tongues entwined, and then she gave in to the urge and bit down.

He pulled away with a yelp of pain, holding his mouth as he glared at her. "What are you doing?"

"I don't want this." Even as she said it, Wendy swayed closer to him, licking her lips.

He eyed her warily. "That's not what your body's saying, but I'm not into these games. If you're saying no, then say it plainly. If you're saying yes, then say that plainly as well."

Wendy wavered with indecision before

really realizing she was acting like the immature one right then after leveling the accusation against him. She was prevaricating and pushing him away even as she tried to pull him closer. She needed to make up her mind. It was time to make a decision and stick with it. Common sense dictated she didn't need to be involved with someone like James Hook. The sensible course was to give him a firm no and resume walking as though they hadn't been lovers for a brief time.

Screw common sense when she so badly wanted to fuck James. "Yes." She spoke the word confidently, and he lunged forward, once more pressing her against the tree.

She was straining against him just as eagerly, and their mouths dueled passionately as their hands roamed freely. She let out a startled gasp when his hands went to the neckline of her tank top and ripped it. She pulled her head away to scowl up at him. "I don't have that many clothes, so what the heck are you doing?"

"I hate seeing Pan's logo on you. You don't belong to him." His brown eye was gleaming, and the cybernetic eye seemed more focused than usual. He completely ripped the tank top from her and then split the fabric into three pieces before tossing it aside. "Never wear that again."

She said, with a hint of irony, "I don't see how I could anyway."

He moved forward, cupping her chin with his hand and forcing her to look at him. "Say it."

"Say what?" She issued the words with an air of challenge as she pressed into him. At the moment, she wasn't certain if they were lovers or adversaries. It felt like some tangled mix of both and was exhilarating, if a bit confusing.

"That you aren't Pan's."

"I was never Peter Pan's. I was *with* him, but I didn't *belong* to him. I don't belong to anyone." Even as she said the words, she recognized the challenge in them, and so did he. She could tell by the way his expression darkened, and the determination that overtook his features. When he kissed her again forcefully, she was ready and waiting for it, responding in kind.

They pulled and pushed at each other, nipping and kissing frantically. Their clothes seemed to disappear with little help, though she was vaguely aware of having stripped his off before he finished undressing her.

She circled her tongue around his nipple before biting hard enough to make him exhale raggedly. She soothed the small hurt with the tip of her tongue before moving to his other nipple to do the same. He grabbed a handful of her hair before she could bite this time, pulling back her head and admonishing her, "Play nice."

She grinned. "Where's the fun in that?"

"It's like that then?" With a little growl, James lifted her into his arms and pressed her against the bark once more. She wrapped her thighs around him, and she was already wet and ready for him when his cock slid inside her, claiming her as his.

She'd never admit it to him, but as they joined, she couldn't help but feel claimed by the Neanderthal side James displayed. It was primal and seductive, and though all kinds of wrong to want to belong to a man, she gladly surrendered herself to his mastery and enjoyed every moment of it as he thrust rapidly into her, bringing her to orgasm twice before surrendering to his own release.

Afterward, they were breathing heavily, but didn't really address what they'd just done. He passed her the white shirt she'd borrowed from him, and she slipped it on. Her nipples were embarrassingly visible now that she no longer had the tank top underneath it, and fluffing out the shirt didn't do much to hide the situation. When she looked up and saw James's gaze on her nipples, she decided not to bother anyway. She liked that hot and hungry look in his eyes, and she couldn't pretend otherwise.

"Right, let's see about lunch, and then

maybe we can get a couple more hours of walking in before we have to stop." James sounded as pragmatic as ever, as though they hadn't just indulged in mind-blowing rough sex against a tree.

Wendy forced her expression to be one of neutrality as she nodded. "Yeah, that's a good plan."

They returned to the place where she'd tried to start a fire before, and this time, Wendy was able to do so in less than a minute. She was relaxed after their bout of rough sex, which should have had the opposite effect. Instead, the encounter left her feeling mellow and had taken away a decent amount of tension between them.

"Oh, my god. Your shoulder." She looked up and saw he was bleeding through the bandage that she'd fashioned.

He looked down and winced. "I guess I wasn't quite up for being ravished by you, Wendy." His eyes, including the blue cybernetic one, sparkled when he told her that.

She rolled her eyes. "I wasn't the one doing the ravishing." That wasn't strictly true though. She recalled how rough she'd been with him, biting and scratching as though determined to mark his flesh and leave some reminder that he belonged to her as much as she belonged to him.

"May I borrow some more of your shirt?"

"Technically, it's your shirt. You ripped mine." She slipped it off and handed it to him. "Try not to cut too much off. I'd like to have some coverage since you've destroyed my tank top."

"Let it go, love." He didn't look at all repentant as he carefully cut off a few inches from the hem and handed it back to her. She slipped it on, finding it impossible to tie now. It hung a few inches below her breasts, but bared her midriff. At least it would stay in place unless a strong breeze blew it up.

"Would you help me with this?" He

held out the makeshift bandage.

Wendy moved to him, trying to find the cleanest section possible before pulling off the old cloth and pressing it against the wound firmly until it stopped bleeding. "I hope we find the *Jolly Roger* today, because I think you need more medicine, and the mallowberry stuff isn't doing enough."

"At least most of the venom is out of my system. I can tell that, because I can think clearly." He remained still and stoic as she carefully rewrapped the wound once the bleeding had slowed to a trickle. "I think we'll find the ship today. I've seen evidence of breakage throughout the tree line, and we've come several miles. I don't think the *Jolly Roger* would've been able to go much farther from where we fell without crashing. There's no way Ceeco would've pressed the ship to its limits if he could find a safe place to land sooner. They wouldn't have wanted to get too far away from us anyway."

Wendy wanted to share his optimism,

so she didn't argue or point out that he could be wrong. Of course he could be wrong, and he likely knew that too. She wanted to believe he was right, so she decided to embrace his optimism, even if it proved to be foolish in the long run.

After preparing their lunch, which tasted unusual, but wasn't terrible, they pressed on. They walked quietly, and she suspected James wasn't feeling up to an expenditure of effort to walk and converse, since he looked pale and slightly sweaty.

For her part, she wasn't ready to talk either, because she didn't know what to say. She didn't even know what to think. She was confused by James, how he made her feel, and the way he tied her up in knots. She was no closer to reaching a determination about how she felt, or what she should do next, when they topped an incline and looked down to see the *Jolly Roger* just a couple of miles away below. Relief filled her, but also a strange sense of dread. Her time alone with James was over, which was probably for the best, but that left her feeling devastated as they increase their pace to reach the ship.

CHAPTER EIGHT

HE WAS FEELING MORE LIGHTHEADED THAN HE WAS letting on, and weakness was edging through him, so it was a relief to reach the *Jolly Roger* a short while later. It was also a disappointment, because it marked the end of his brief time alone with Wendy, and he had no idea what the future held for them.

He was pleased as he walked around

the ship to see the breaches had been sealed, and other damage had been repaired. The ship looked a bit piecemeal at the moment, but it appeared to be structurally sound. He knocked on the closed door after examining the ship, leaning heavily against the side for a moment. He didn't miss Wendy's discreet attempt to support him as she moved closer, letting him lean against her.

He hated to accept the offer and show weakness, but displaying vulnerability with Wendy felt different than it did with anyone else. He wasn't her captain, or expected to be in command and control at all times.

He was her lover, though they hadn't established how long that situation would last. The logical thing would be to end it now that they were back with the ship and would soon be leaving the planet— but his heart wasn't listening to his logical brain at the moment. The thought of giving her up sent a pain through him that was unmatched even by the dull burning in his shoulder.

The door lowered to make the gangplank a moment later, and Smee stood there. He beamed at them. "James, it's good to see you. And you too, Miss Wendy. We were so worried when you fell out of the ship."

"We landed in hot water," said Wendy.

Smee nodded. "There was trouble?"

James laughed. "Yes, but Wendy means we actually landed in hot water. We hit a lake, or perhaps an ocean, but it was still in the stages of terraforming. It wasn't acidic, but was hot. Still, it was a better landing spot than the ground." He swayed suddenly, and Wendy put her arm around his waist. James ignored Smee's cocked brow at that gesture. "As for the trouble, we ran into some kind of beastie." He used his good hand to wave to his injured shoulder. "I could use some medicine."

"Of course, James." Smee scrambled down the gangplank, coming around on his other side to support his arm and shoulder carefully as they guided him up the gangplank. James felt ridiculous requiring their assistance, but he was also feeling almost as weak as a baby. He probably shouldn't have pushed himself to start walking again so soon after the injury, but it had worked out for the best now that they were back at the ship.

They led him to the makeshift medical bay, where they stocked the basics and a little more, but none of the crew was a doctor, so there wasn't much reason to keep more serious things on hand. Fortunately, they had a laser suture kit and some medicines, and Smee fixed him up.

James noted that Wendy remained beside him throughout, squeezing his hand. She seemed to be feeling the pain more acutely than he was, and he wasn't certain whether to be amused or moved. He ended up feeling both. He doubted his Wendy even realized what she was betraying, or how vulnerable she was making herself with her emotions. He vowed to do nothing to damage those emotions as Smee gave him a hypodermic injection a short time later. James was already feeling a lot better, and part of that was seeing how Wendy felt.

"Give me a status report, Smee." As he spoke, he stood up over Wendy's objections and ignored Smee's steadying hand. Resting and getting proper medical care had made a big difference. He wasn't ready to run through the jungle for hours, but he could stand and walk to the bridge of the ship on his own two feet.

"We've been busy, and Cecco's been working himself round-the-clock. He has almost everything repaired, except the ansible. He's hoping to have that up and running by this afternoon, so we can send out a call to the rest of the crew to rendezvous somewhere."

"How damaged was the ship?" asked Wendy.

"Oh, she took a beating," said Smee. "Ceeco had quite the task ahead of him when we first crashed. I helped, but I don't know half the things he does, and he seems to know it all on instinct."

"But where did you get parts?" Wendy looked around, as though expecting a spaceship repair station to materialize.

"We keep many on hand," said James. "It's not always possible to stop at a planet to get repairs when we have bounties on our head and the ship. There are limited places where we're welcome among friends, so it makes more sense to carry our own inventory with us. I think we have enough supplies that, with Ceeco's knowledge, we could probably replicate the *Jolly Roger* if we needed to." That was a slight exaggeration, but they clearly had the things they needed on hand, and the *Jolly Roger* was likely to be underway within a few hours.

"Ceeco's in the communications area of the engine room. I'll go fetch him, James."

James settled into his seat on the bridge and waved a hand. "There's no need. Let him finish what he's working on, and perhaps lend a hand." It was James's not-so-subtle attempt to tell Smee he wanted to be alone with Wendy. Fortunately, Smee was quick on the uptake and a clever man, which was part of the reason they were such good friends. With a nod in his direction, and a slight bow toward Wendy, Smee left them.

Wendy stood beside him, looking awkward. Giving in to impulse, he took her hand and pulled her down onto his lap. She was stiff with resistance for a moment, but then melted against him. She laid her head on his chest and whispered in a loving tone, "Don't read too much into this, Hook."

"Of course not, Darling." He wrapped his arms around her to hold her closer.

They were silent for a bit before she asked, "We have a little while to wait?" At his nod, Wendy continued, "In that case, why don't you tell me how you became a pirate?"

"Have you forgotten about Bones taking me on?"

She sighed. "No, of course not. I'd like

to know what circumstances led up to that. How did you become a pirate, or how did you end up in that situation where it became a feasible option?"

James thought about refusing to explain, but decided he owed Wendy that much. Just because he didn't enjoy talking about it didn't mean she didn't deserve to hear his past. "You have to understand the long, complicated history of the Hook descendants and the Navy. We started with the British Navy and the ocean, but Hooks, particularly Hook men, all do at least a short enlistment in Naval service."

"All of them?"

He nodded. "Every single one for the past twenty generations. My father is a retired admiral, so I was going to follow in his footsteps. I had my career planned out, and I was determined to serve with honor to make my father and the Coalition proud." There was a heavy hint of melancholy in his tone as he spoke the words, allowing himself a brief moment to remember the idealistic and naïve young man he'd been once upon a time.

"What happened?"

"I followed orders blindly, which was what I was trained to do, but common sense should have asserted itself. Admiral Tikta Croc, a man I considered something of a mentor, put in a call for assistance, and he wanted us to come quietly and discreetly. My ship then was the *Dauntless*, and we slipped in silently to the planet from where Croc's call had originated.

"We discovered them fighting a heavily armed garrison of soldiers, and we provided the support required. We were outnumbered, and it looked like we would lose at one point, so Smee called for reinforcements. After that, we turned the tide and subdued them. When the Admiral discovered Smee's call, he became livid. I didn't understand why, at least until Coalition forces arrived.

"Before that, Croc mercilessly executed every one of the Kloptin soldiers on the planet that we had managed to defeat in the interim. I was opposed, but he ignored my counsel, and it never occurred to me to mutiny on behalf of people I thought had started the aggression. At least the thought didn't occur to me then. All I did was record what was happening discreetly. Cecco was the one who thought to take the prototype and hide it. He didn't tell me until months later, after the trial and court-martialing."

"What prototype?"

He didn't answer her question for, since his thoughts were on the dematerializer. "The technology existed, but wasn't working. Croc went through all that subterfuge and murder to steal non-working technology." He let out a bitter laugh.

"He wasn't there officially, was he?" Wendy was tense in his arms.

James pulled Wendy a little closer to him. "No, but I didn't know that at the time. It was some black-ops mission. He received intel that it was a research planet working on dematerialization technology, which the Coalition has been after for years. Since the Kloptins weren't Coalition-aligned, Croc thought he could just help himself to the technology."

She squeezed his hand tightly, still seeming to be caught up in the intrigue. "For what purpose?"

He shrugged. "To this day, I have no idea if Croc planned to turn it over to the Coalition or sell it to the highest bidder. What he discovered when he got there was far more than a research station. There was also a military outpost, and he met with stiff resistance. He called me in, thinking I could be persuaded to keep my mouth shut. If Smee hadn't called for backup, there's no telling what event would have been recorded in our logs, if any appeared at all." He hung his head in shame for a moment. "The worst part is, I probably would've gone along with it in my need to follow orders."

Wendy shook her head. "I don't think you would've."

"I didn't even release the footage of

him executing the Kloptin soldiers, Wendy." He let out a sigh. "You have to understand how idealistic I was then. I was determined to be the perfect officer and the perfect captain. I wanted to please my father and remain the perfect son. I didn't deviate from orders, and I certainly didn't think for myself back then. You can imagine what a rude awakening it was when Coalition forces arrived, and Croc told them I had been the one attacking the planet, and he answered our distress call only to discover the truth of why I was there afterward.

"I protested, but no one believed me over the admiral with his illustrious career." He closed his eyes for a moment, recalling the flash of betrayal when his own father had refused to listen to him. "I tried showing the recording, but they refused to view it. Croc confiscated it, not knowing Smee had made a backup while we awaited the Coalition forces. He was less naïve than me and had an inkling of what was going to happen."

She scowled. "They wouldn't even view the footage?"

James shook his head. "They refused and claimed it was irrelevant. I think they didn't want to have to arrest Croc and bring to light his illegal operations, so they decided to let me take the fall." Better James Hook than Bartholomew Hook. He was convinced that had been the thinking of those in the know.

"Bastards. What did they do?"

"I was arrested, and they court-martialed me. They court-martialed Smee and Ceeco as well, since they were my closest officers and implicated in Croc's accusation. We were split up and sent to different penal colonies, but I managed to escape along the way. Instead of going after Smee and Ceeco, who were sent to a different place, I let anger blind me."

Wendy's fingers danced lightly over his prosthetic hand, and he reflexively tightened his fingers around them to hold her. "Is that when you lost your hand? You mentioned your bid for revenge earlier, and that the person who took your hand was going to feed you to his fish."

He nodded. "I confronted Croc without a lick of sense. He was surrounded by his people, and I was outnumbered. I got in a couple of good punches, but then they held me while he cut off my hand. Fortunately for me, Smee and Ceeco had managed to escape with the help of Cookson and Turley, who bribed the guards on the prison ship to let them go. The four of them rescued me and got me out of there, and then we drifted together until meeting up with old Bones almost a year later. When I had the money, I had my hand replaced, and I became a pirate captain."

"But you were the dashing Coalition captain first." There was a hint of wistfulness in her tone, and her eyes were shining. She was clearly idealizing the bold hero she pictured he'd been.

In good conscience, James couldn't allow her to continue doing that. "I was once, but that guy is gone. He might as well be dead, and what you see now—the roguish pirate captain, who plunders and steals for a living—that's me. This is James Hook, not that idiot who blindly followed."

Wendy licked her lips before lifting her head to brush them against his. "You might as well know I have a thing for bad boys. I find the idea of you being a Coalition captain dashing and kind of sexy, but I like this version of James Hook far better." As she spoke, her hand moved to the waistband of his pants to slip inside, and he groaned when she started stroking him. "Why don't you plunder me while we have some time to kill, Captain Hook?"

Since James couldn't think of a reason why he shouldn't, he did exactly that. Wendy was soon screaming his name, which reverberated around the bridge, and likely alerted Smee and Ceeco what was taking place in the room. He hoped so, to keep them from entering, because if they walked in at the moment, they would see their pirate captain letting Wendy ride him in the captain's chair.

1

It took a little longer than Ceeco had estimated, but they were able to launch the *Jolly Roger* off the planet that night. James was on alert, and he could tell Wendy was on edge as well. She was lingering near him, refusing to leave the bridge even when he suggested she go lie down in his room. Instead, she seemed to want to be near him, and he was feeling the same way.

The ship was sound as ever, so it was smooth sailing as they plotted a course to Ceeco's home planet. He tasked Smee with the mission of sending out communications to the men who were scattered in the life pods to rendezvous on Vakreet, which was a familiar planet to all the crew.

The Vlorn had no great love for the Coalition despite their status as a

Coalition member. Ceeco had explained to him that they had been co-opted into the Coalition, mainly because their people were so skilled with technology. They all chafed under Coalition rule, so when it came to assisting the pirate captain to whom their son was so loyal, the Ceccos had no problem doing so.

They were a port in the storm, and James was happy to have them available—and made a habit of not taking advantage of their hospitality too often. He didn't want to endanger them, and he didn't want to wear out his welcome.

They landed at the Ceeco homestead on Vakreet when it was dark. Juud Ceeco, who was Cecco's father, was the only one who came to greet them since it was so late. He welcomed them to the planet and invited them inside his home. James declined the invitation to sleep in their dwellings, since they had the ship.

"What about you, miss?" asked Juud of Wendy.

Wendy sent James an uncertain look

before shaking her head. "I'll stay with him. Thanks."

Juud nodded before turning to his son. "Andony, you'll come in, won't you? Your mother would be slighted if you didn't share our dwelling and sleep in your old room."

Andony nodded, looking slightly embarrassed, but clearly not going to let possible ribbing from his crewmates allow him to disappoint his mother.

"Everyone will rest this evening, and we'll discuss the situation tomorrow," said Juud with a nod to all of them. Andony followed him into the dwelling, and James and the rest of the crew returned to the *Jolly Roger*. Wendy was right beside him, and there was no debate when he took her hand and led her to his room.

James had every intention of just going to sleep for a few hours, but she was too tempting, and it was impossible not to make love before they ended up falling asleep together. As he held her while she slept, James accepted that she was his. He had no intention of letting Wendy Darling walk out of his life, but he also wasn't ready to share that with her. He was afraid she would object or escape on principle, and he wanted a chance to woo her and convince her to stay.

Chapter Nine

Wendy woke without James beside her the next morning and had a moment of panic. That she reacted so strongly to his mere absence was telling, and she collapsed against the pillows again as she tried to breathe through the second round of panic, which was spurred by how integral he was becoming to her existence.

How could she be falling for him, and

so fast? He was all wrong for her—except he felt so right. Being with him felt right, and the sex was amazing. They couldn't spend all their time in bed though, and anything she thought she was feeling was bound to fall apart with enough time. Right? That she wasn't completely certain worried her, but she couldn't maintain the panic as she adapted to the idea that she was falling for James.

He was exciting and lived a life full of danger. That appealed to her after years of drudgery and familial duty. She loved her brothers and grandmother, but wanted more from life than being Johnny and Mikey's stand-in mother, or forgetful Nana's caretaker. The life James led would never be dull, and she enjoyed the idea of being a pirate's wench. Even better, he could take care of himself and could also take care of her when she needed someone to lean on. She wasn't looking for someone to watch over her, but she liked the idea of not being the one responsible for everyone else's needs for a change.

Too bad it came with a life of being on the run and on the edge of danger. She knew she should regard those things as negatives when evaluating a future with James, but her heart raced with anticipation instead. She might as well face it. She was getting emotionally invested in him.

Just as she was accepting that epiphany, James entered his room and marched over to the bed. With his hands on his hips, he stared down at her with a disapproving look, which the gleam in his eyes completely ruined. "Still abed, lazy bones? Get up and dress, love. We have work to do." His gaze flicked to her bracelet before returning to her.

"I'll be up in a minute." She was naked under the bedding and not anxious to flash anyone who might pass, since James had left the door open.

As though he'd read her thoughts, he reached down and plucked off the bedding. He waggled his eyebrows with lustful appreciation as he trailed a hand down the curve of her breast before tweaking the nipple. "Or perhaps I should join you for a nap?"

Wendy snorted. "I doubt much sleeping will take place." She picked up his pillow and tossed it at him. "Give me some privacy to dress in peace—and don't forget to leave the door open, since it won't recognize my biometric profile to let me out otherwise."

He strode to the door and closed it with him still inside. She'd meant to dress alone, but just shook her head as she got out of bed, deciding she could control herself for a short time—at least long enough not to tear off his clothes and ravish him. There would be time for that later.

Unless he took her straight back to New London. The thought filled her with dread and almost made her desperate enough to throw herself at him and plead for him to let her stay. The humiliation of doing so held her back, and she stood in the center of the room for a moment, looking for her clothes. She was about to ask James where they were when he came toward her.

He took her hand and pulled her gently behind him. "Let's fix that."

"Fix what? And where are my clothes?"

James lifted the hand he still held and pressed it to the biometric panel before authorizing the computer to add her profile to the crew list. Wendy grew unexpectedly choked up at the gesture, since it seemed to be implying there was some kind of future with him and the crew. She swallowed the urge to bawl and lifted her hand when he nodded. "Thanks. Now...clothes?"

"I threw those out."

She scowled. "I can't stay in here naked or walk around in a bedsheet, Hook."

His lips twitched. "Ah, back to Hook again. Don't worry, my sweet. Andony's sisters gifted you a few things."

Wendy looked down at her naked body reflexively. "Are they Vlorn?"

"They're half-Vlorn. One of their mothers is a Kloptin, and the other is human." He frowned. "Why? Do you have an issue with wearing Vlorn clothing?" He seemed on the verge of rebuking her for that view.

She shook her head. "Of course not, but Cecco, er, Andony, is tall and broad. If his sisters are built like him, I don't see how anything they loan me could fit."

He blinked and then grinned, looking relieved. "They're both smaller than their brothers, but if you have issues, Smee can help modify the fit. His father was a tailor for the Coalition uniform depot, and he picked up some things."

"Oh, good." She moved closer to put her arms around him. "How can I thank you for your thoughtfulness?" Wendy deliberately rubbed her breasts against him.

He cleared his throat. "Many and varied ways, which will have to wait. Juud is expecting us."

She sighed and stepped back. "In that

case, where are the clothes?"

"In your half of the closet." He stated it so casually, as though it didn't mean anything that he had designated half his closet for her. That didn't sound like the action of someone who planned to get rid of her as soon as he could.

She tried to hide her idiotic grin as she walked to the closet and selected some of the garments. The shirts were a bit too long, though manageable, but the pants were fine once she tucked them into her boots, and she joined James a few moments later.

Together, they left the Jolly Roger and walked across the land belonging to the Ceccos. It was verdant and filled with plants and animals. Wendy found it too bucolic after living on New London, but it had a certain charm.

James led her into a large building which appeared to be a workshop. Juud waited for them in the center of the room and waved for Wendy to take a seat on a metal chair. "I've prepared a batch of nanites to short-circuit the bracelet's security system, so please place your hand here." He gestured to a tube-like structure.

Wendy sat and eyed it dubiously. "Will it hurt?"

"Not at all," said Juud.

"Will I have those things in me when you're done?"

Juud's craggy face radiated confidence. "Not at all," he repeated.

"How do you know for sure?" Wendy was skeptical about having nanotech, though she knew many people who had it and claimed it made life easier.

"They're drawn to a certain frequency and will return to the collector when I emit it."

He seemed confident, and she'd promised to cooperate, so she put her hand in the tube, which extended partway up her forearm. There was a flash and a quiet hum that lasted less than a minute.

"Scan's clear. No nanites remain, so

you can pull out your arm."

Following Juud's instructions, she did so, almost expecting to see a stump, or something else dramatic to herald it had all gone wrong. Instead, she saw her bare wrist, and the bracelet lay in the tube. She reached in again to retrieve it and pass it to James.

He eyed it closely, bringing it near his cybernetic eye.

She frowned. "What are you doing?"

"I'm scanning the chip to get the location of where he hid the loot," said James in a distracted way.

Wendy's eyes widened. "If you can do that, why didn't you just scan the bracelet while it was on my wrist?"

He froze and looked startled for a moment. Then he stammered, "I didn't have time to do that on Neverland."

She shrugged. "Maybe not then, but during the last few days? It doesn't..." She trailed off before saying it didn't make sense. It took every ounce of control not to. beam idiotically when she realized

James hadn't thought about reading it before, and the most likely reason was he wanted an excuse, perhaps influenced by his subconscious, to keep her with him. Or was she reading too much into it?

Stealing a peek at him from the corner of her eye, she saw he had flushed a ruddy color and looked disconcerted even in the midst of examining the chip in the bracelet. Perhaps he'd reached the same conclusion and was absorbing the truth— he could have been rid of her days ago if he'd really wanted to be.

She decided not to flog the point and instead chatted with Juud for a bit. He showed her some of his tools and explained he was the one who had designed James's cybernetic eye and sensor system.

"It's lightyears ahead of most available tech," said James as he held out the bracelet to her. "Do you want this back now?"

She snorted. "It was a gift from Peter, so no. I thought it had sentimental value, but now I'm sure it only held monetary value. He probably thought it would be safe on my wrist, since the cutthroats he called friends wouldn't be able to take it off." She blanched. "I wonder if he realized any one of them would have gladly cut off my hand to get the microchip if they'd known what it held?"

"Knowing Pan, it was an acceptable risk. He's motivated by self-interest." James made the character indictment in a scathing tone.

She nodded emphatically before pausing. "You never did tell me how you knew Peter, you know?"

He sighed before nodding to Juud. "Take a walk with me?"

She fell into step beside him, and they wandered onto the fertile land surrounding the structures. "So...?" she prompted after a few moments of silence.

"Peter Pan came to me with the deal of a lifetime. He needed help executing the robbery of a Coalition treasury, and I had inside knowledge, along with a competent crew. It so happened this treasury was filled with platinum and rhodium bars that were unmarked. A little digging revealed this stash was under Croc's personal control for his black-ops activities, so there's no official record of its existence." He grinned, and it held no mercy. Only vicious joy for a moment that was somehow sexy on him.

"I assume that appealed to your need for revenge?" she asked.

"Of course. Pan isn't stupid and probably realized it would lure me into working with someone I barely knew. He double-crossed me in the end. It wasn't anywhere close to honorable either. He suggested we two captains should be the only ones in the vault, to safeguard it from our crews until we determined the value. I knew I could trust my people, but didn't trust his, so I agreed." His voice was thick with anger.

"What did he do to you?"

James ran a hand through his long hair to push it off his face and point to the scar there. "He slashed my face with his sword and took my left eye when he attacked me from the side while I knelt down to pull out bars, leaving me bleeding in the vault we'd robbed. My crew interceded and rescued me before the Coalition could respond to the soldiers' SOS, and I made it my mission to track down Pan to get the treasure. He buried it, but we're going to find it. The amount of credits involved is staggering. Things will be different for all of us when we find it."

Wendy was warmed that he seemed to be including her in the *us* he mentioned. "What's your plan now?"

"Retrieve my treasure." He smiled. "But first, the Ceccos are hosting a celebration dinner for us this evening, so prepare to feast, drink, and dance."

"And be ravished?" she whispered as she leaned close enough that her lips brushed the side of his when she spoke.

"Of course, love." He kissed her passionately before pulling away. "I have things to do before the celebration, but

I'll see you this evening. Tula and Yorka have already invited you to join them in the main dwelling if you'd like to visit or help with preparations."

"They're Andony's sisters?"

James nodded before pointing her in the right direction. He swatted her bottom as she walked past him. "Until this evening, Wendy." He gave her a look full of desire.

She reciprocated in full as she hurried to the Ceccos' dwelling. Curiosity had her wondering what James's plan was to retrieve the treasure, but she didn't pry just yet. She would ask him later and see where she fit into the plan.

I

THE celebration was well under way, and Wendy was pleasantly mellow after imbibing a generous amount of some fermented beverage called *mec* that reminded her of lavender and lemons, but was a faint blue color. The food had been excellent as well, and now the Ceccos and some of their neighbors gathered in the front of their homestead to play music and dance.

She sat on a bench by herself, watching the others. Her gaze kept returning to James, who was currently dancing with Yorka, the youngest Cecco child at just fifteen planet rotations. She was trying to teach him a complicated step, and he was a good sport.

She grinned as he spun Yorka, who was clearly giggling breathlessly when she returned to him. The look of adoration on her face revealed her crush, but James seemed to have struck the right balance between making her feel special without crossing any lines. He had a way with the females of the species.

No wonder she was falling in love with him.

Wendy was in the process of sipping the *mec* when the thought hit her. She gasped and choked on a fiery mouthful that burned all the way down. Smee turned to helpfully pound her back, and she couldn't manage to wave away his "help" for a moment. When she caught her breath and thanked him, she figured she'd end up with bruises on her back from the prolonged pounding.

Once the shock of choking passed, the shock of her thought took prominence, and she tried to deny she'd even had it. Of course she wasn't falling for James. That would be ridiculous—except it didn't feel ridiculous. It felt...right. There was no other way around it but to accept the truth. She was on her way to loving him if she didn't pull back, and she had no wish to thwart her burgeoning emotions from continuing to grow.

Before she had a chance to really process, James stood before her. He extended a hand to pull her onto the makeshift dance floor and started teaching her the steps Yorka had shown him. Wendy tried to keep up, but her head was spinning. She didn't think she'd drunk enough *mec* to use that as the excuse, so it had to be James himself, along with the recent realization of her strong feelings.

When he spun her as he'd done Yorka, she stumbled, and he quickly lifted her off her feet and held her against him. Wendy wrapped her arms around him and held tightly even after she'd regained her balance.

"Are you steady now?"

She shook her head.

He frowned. "The dance isn't that complicated."

Wendy quirked half her mouth into a small grin. "It's extremely complicated, but I don't think that's going to stop me." She knew they were talking about different things.

He looked a little confused. "Shall we try the spin step again?"

She stretched her head a bit to kiss him. "You can make my head spin in a much better way, James."

His eyes widened, and he looked around for a moment. "It might be rude to slip away."

"Dinner is over, and now it's dancing and socializing. I don't think they'll miss us."

He hesitated one more moment before nodding and setting her on her feet. "Dance toward the perimeter of the group, and we'll slip into the shadows when we can."

Wendy followed his directions, and it took about ten minutes of maneuvering through the dancers to reach an area near the shadows. They darted toward them together, hands entwined, and James didn't release her even after they were alone and moved farther from the party.

They walked for a bit without speaking, until reaching a growth of trees that sheltered them from view of the party. "Would you prefer a bed?" asked James.

Wendy turned to face him, pushing him against a tree in a move similar to the one he'd used on her while they were on the terraformed planet. She started out aggressive and needy, but he was holding back.' No, not holding back. Just going slowly and being tender, especially with his drugging kisses.

His way quickly won her over, and she gentled her touch and slowed her pace. Wendy dropped to her knees before him after undoing his gun belt and trousers. He moaned softly when she wafted her moist mouth over his cock without fully engaging. His hands dug into her hair, which she wore unrestrained at the moment, to tug her closer with care.

Wendy opened her mouth and gripped the base of his shaft with one hand, using it to guide him into her mouth. He moaned again as she took him to the back of her throat, slowly rubbing him with her tongue before she began sucking and moving her head back and forward. He was at her mercy and seemed happy to surrender. She was thrilled to give him this gift. She'd never done this with anyone before, but it no longer seemed faintly repulsive. She wanted to please him and make it perfect.

He trembled as he thrust into her until

he breached the back of her throat. He grunted when she moaned and swallowed automatically, and his hand tightened in her hair to hold her against him. When she swallowed again, he twitched before spilling inside her mouth. Wendy swallowed every drop before carefully disengaging her mouth and sitting on her shins. She looked up at him to gauge his reaction. His heavy-lidded look spoke of pure satisfaction as he leaned heavily against the tree.

She stood up, letting out a squeal of surprise when James turned her around to pull the dress Tula had loaned her above her waist. She wore no panties, since the girls had none to fit her, so she was bared to him. She yelped when he pushed her forward, until she was on the ground, but her knees were on a tree stump. He knelt behind her, burying his face between her thighs, and his tongue thrust into her. She wiggled, wanting more, and he increased the pace as he thrust his tongue in and out of her.

"James, more," she whispered, struggling to keep her voice low to avoid detection.

He didn't say anything, but his mouth became fast and wicked, bringing her an intense orgasm that faded into another. Before she could regain any semblance of control from that one, he entered her from behind and thrust forcefully into her.

Wendy pushed back against him, needing every inch he gave her. She wanted to become one with him, and though it wasn't possible, they found a close approximation as they moved together in their shared need. When his cock twitched inside her a bit later, she was already on the verge of coming again and slipped over the edge with a keening cry.

His hand moved over her mouth to silence her, but he was making small sounds himself as he emptied inside her and held her tenderly for the next few minutes. She leaned forward, placing her head on her crossed forearms, and struggled to regain her composure.

"Wendy?"

"Yes, James."

"That was amazing."

She chuckled. "Mmhmm. I could stay like this forever."

"About that..."

She braced herself to hear something awful from his hesitant tone. "What?"

"This is putting a terrible kink in my back. I know that makes me sound old, but—"

She dissolved into giggles as he pulled out of her and stood up. She was still laughing when he helped her to her feet and turned her to face him. She leaned against him as she quelled her mirth. "Oh, James. That was the most perfect moment."

"Until I ruined it," he said with a self-deprecating grimace.

She cupped his face in her hands. "Not at all. It was still perfect. So perfect that I'd like to try it in a real bed now."

"That's easily arranged." He rushed her from the forested area and back to the homestead. They slipped discreetly onto the *Jolly Roger* and straight to James's quarters, where they found a different kind of pleasure in slow and easy lovemaking that made Wendy more certain than ever that she was falling for James, and there was no turning back now.

1

ONCE more, she woke alone, but without James there to ensure she was up. She slid out of bed and showered before dressing. Then she went looking for him, but didn't have to go far. He and his crew were near the ship looking at a 3D holomap of the plotted galaxies. He was pointing toward a small green dot in the vast image when she came to stand beside him. She put her arm around his waist without thought until he stiffened. She immediately dropped her arm, feeling an unspoken censure. After a moment, he took her hand and brought it to his mouth to kiss the back of it before dropping their joined hands to their sides. When she started to pull away, he clung tighter.

Feeling buoyed and reassured, she gestured toward the map. "What's this? Peter's map?"

"Yes, Miss Wendy," said Smee. "The green dot is where he hid the treasure."

She whistled. "It's far away, isn't it?"

James grunted. "It's almost on the other side of the galaxy from his hideout. I expected him to be more paranoid and keep it closer. I'd half-hoped it would be on Neverland, but it couldn't be that easy." His expression twisted into sourness.

"We're heading out in a bit to retrieve it," said Andony.

"Do I have time to thank your family for their hospitality first?" asked Wendy.

"Yes," said Andony.

"No," said James at the same time.

She gave him a curious look. "No?"

"I mean, there's no need. You'll be

staying here."

Wendy scowled. Her hands went to her hips as she looked briefly at the crew. "I need a few moments alone with your captain." She said the words sternly, daring defiance, and received none. The men scattered in seconds. They might not have been so cooperative if James had countermanded her, but he remained silent.

When they were gone, she turned to James and poked him in the chest. "What do you think you're doing? We had a deal, remember? You owe me a ride to New London." She started to poke him again for emphasis.

James intercepted her hand, holding it with a bit of force to keep her from finishing her trajectory. "I remember, and I plan to give you a ride home when we return, if that's where you want to go." He scowled for a moment before his expression blanked. "The mission to retrieve the treasure will be dangerous, if it's still there. Pan has a head start, and it's quite likely he's already loaded it and diverted it somewhere else during the time we were stranded on the planet."

She pointed to their current location with her free hand. "We've come farther though. We're closer than he would be from Neverland."

He sighed. "But he could have left Neverland just behind us. I don't want you hurt." There was no denying his earnestness.

Wendy shrugged. "I don't want you hurt either, but I'm not asking you to stay behind. You can't ask that of me either. In fact, I'm practically part of your crew and demand my share."

His eyes narrowed, and he looked like he'd argue for a moment before giving her a slow grin instead. "If I accept you onto my crew, that means you have to obey me."

She frowned. "I should get an exemption because we're sleeping together."

James laughed. "It won't work that

way. Do you agree to obey me?"

Wendy hesitated before nodding. "Yes, but only on crew and captain stuff. Our personal life is separate from our working relationship."

"Agreed, but I do reserve the right to dole out unusual punishments unique to you." He started to walk toward the ship, and since he was still holding her hand, he was propelling her forward.

She dug her heels into the dirt. "Wait."

He slowed down, but didn't stop.

"Dammit, Hook, stop."

Her irritation seemed to get through to him, because he turned to face her. "Yes, Ensign Darling?" His twitching lips revealed how much he was enjoying this.

"What kind of punishment?"

"The usual for infractions is time in the brig or worse."

She cocked a brow. "How much worse?"

"Lashings for serious rule-breaking that endangers the crew."

Wendy flinched. "If that's usual, what

would you do to me?"

He lifted the hand he held to trail his tongue over her knuckles. "I could never mar the lovely flesh of your back."

She let out a sigh of relief that was short-lived.

"Instead, I would turn your ass red with my hand before fucking you until you're screaming my name." He spoke the words casually.

She blinked. "Oh."

His lips twitched again, and this time, Wendy noticed he'd cropped his beard and mustache. "There would be Os involved too, I'm sure. Do you accept these conditions, Ensign Darling?"

She scowled. "Just Wendy, if you please."

"Oh, I'm well pleased with just Wendy." He nibbled on her knuckle. "Accept."

With a grudging nod, she said, "I accept."

He gave her a smile that had a definite predatory edge. "I shouldn't encourage you to break rules or step outside the chain-of-command, but I anticipate the first time you do so."

Wendy firmed her shoulders. "I won't make any mistakes." She spoke more confidently than she felt.

He threw back his head and laughed. "Of course you won't. Come along, Just Wendy. We need to catch up with Pan, and fortunately, the *Jolly Roger* is one of the fastest ships around, thanks to Cecco. We might pull this off."

She went along with him, finding his enthusiasm contagious. That was tempered slightly by the thoughts filling of her mind of him disciplining her. She could picture being across his lap as he smacked her bottom until it was red. She writhed slightly and wasn't sure whether she was more afraid or turned on by the possible scenario. She wouldn't deliberately break any rules during such an important mission, but she also hadn't ruled out the possibility of doing so in the future, when there was far less at stake, just to see her punishment.

Chapter Ten

It took two days to reach the planet where Pan had stashed their treasure. It had no name and wasn't technically considered part of Coalition territory. Though they made good time, James wasn't at all surprised when they entered orbit of the planet and Cecco said, "There's already a ship down there, and I think it's the *Pixie Dust*, Captain."

"Of course." James sighed.

Wendy moved to closer to him, and her scent made his heart race despite his need to focus on the issue at hand.

"What'll you do now, James?"

"There's just the one ship, Ceeco?"

"Aye, Captain"

"And just seven lifeforms," added Smee.

"In that case, we're going to set down right in front of them. The *Pixie Dust* is no match for the *Jolly Roger*, and we have a few more crewmembers than they do. Pan probably won't expect us to face him head-on, since he would pull some kind of sneaky trick, so that gives us an edge. Take us down, Mr. Ceeco."

Wendy moved even closer to him, and he noticed her hair was back in the braid today. Surreptitiously, he reached out and grasped a handful of it, wrapping it around his fist several times. He liked the symbolism of holding onto her, and he also found the silky softness of her hair reassuring. Arousing too, but now was hardly the time to deal with that.

She whispered, "You aren't going to be hurt, are you?"

"I wasn't sure you'd care, Wendy." He said the word lightly, regretting them when she flinched.

"I would." She bit out the words, adding nothing to them, but she appeared upset.

He wasn't certain if she was angry with his teasing, or if she was genuinely dwelling on the fear of him being injured.

He pulled his gaze from the vid screen for a moment to face her, cupping her chin and angling it upward when she refused to look at him. He waited until she made eye contact before speaking quietly. "The day Peter Pan gets one over me is the day I deserve to be defeated. We're all going to be safe, so don't worry. Promise you'll be safe as well—and listen to my every command."

She nodded grudgingly, and he released her chin. "I'm still not sure about listening to your orders."

"I'm a skilled captain, and I know what's best." James could barely keep in a chuckle at her outraged expression when he tried to claim that. Fortunately for him, they had passed through the atmosphere and were approaching the landing spot. "Get us as close to the *Pixie Dust* as you can. Better yet if you manage to block them in so they can't take off. Make sure we can escape, of course."

Ceeco nodded, and the ship slowed to landing speed. As they covered the last few hundred meters to the ground, Hook chuckled when Smee changed the view of the vid screen to home in on where Pan and his crew were busy loading.

"What's funny?" asked Wendy, who still seemed worried.

"Pan's wearing his brown pants. How perfect." He turned away for a moment to look at her as the crew around him snickered at his crude joke. Wendy was the only one who appeared oblivious, and he didn't bother to explain it for her. "Buck up and follow orders, Ensign

234

Darling, and we'll all be fine."

Wendy looked desperate to believe him, though still uncertain. The fact that she didn't have complete faith in him prickled more than it should, but he also knew he had to prove to her why he was the captain and capable of leading— including leading her.

The ship set down, and they were on the planet moments later. It was barren and desolate, with barely enough oxygen levels to support them, so they wore discreet nasal respirators to augment the levels of oxygen on the planet.

James took the lead, striding toward Pan's crew with his laser rifle extended in their direction. Everyone around him was armed similarly, including Turley, though he also had his sword on his back. Even Wendy had a small laser pistol from his personal collection.

He paused a few feet from Pan, directing his gun at him and ignoring Peter's ineffectual laser sword. "Step away from the treasure and unload your ship."

"We had a deal," whined Pan. "A fifty-fifty split."

"That was before you double-crossed me and cut out my eye, Pan. You're lucky if I let you go with your life. Do as I say."

"You can't just give in," said Tink. "You're stronger than that, Peter."

Wendy snorted, and James barely managed to hide a smile at her response. Pan's reaction didn't help him control his mirth either, because he looked wounded and offended all at once.

"You can't have it," said Pan in an authoritative tone. Too bad the knocking of his knobby knees ruined his show of command.

James rolled his eyes. "Unload your ship now, and I'll allow you to fly away from here with it still intact. If we have to unload it, I'll destroy the *Pixie Dust* before we leave, and you'll be stranded here." James projected his own authoritative tone, and this one made Pan and most of Pan's crew flinch. Only Tink wasn't smart enough to respond to the promise of violence in his tone.

She shoved at Peter's arm. "Fight him, Peter."

Peter took a step back, edging away from James. "I don't think that's a good idea, Tink. It's obvious what's going to have to happen here."

Tink let out a sound of impatience. "You can't seriously plan to give him our treasure?"

"My treasure," corrected James.

She glared at him. "That's enough out of you, Hook. You can't have our treasure."

"If Peter's like his usual self, you won't get much anyway, Tink. What is it he gives you these days? About one-seventeenth, isn't it? And yet, when you count his closest cohorts, he has just six, including you. Does that strike you as fair?" Wendy issued the words as she stepped forward to stand beside James.

Her shoulder was touching his, and he wondered if it was a deliberate show of solidarity, or if she was simply drawn to him the way he was drawn to her and needed to touch her whenever she was in his vicinity.

"I don't want to hear anything from you, Darling." Tink glared at Wendy. "It's not your business and never was."

"Ladies, let's settle down. I'm sure we can come to an arrangement." Pan flashed what was probably supposed to be a charming grin.

He winked at Wendy, and James took an involuntary step forward in response. He had the urge to rip Pan apart with his bare hands despite his proffered guarantee of allowing them to leave the planet with their ship whole, albeit their cargo hold empty of the treasure.

"I can see your point, James, so how about this? You take three-fourths of the loot, and my crew and me and Wendy will just fly away from here. That way, we get a share as well, since you have to concede that my crew did at least half the work to get this vast treasure, and you wouldn't have known about it at all without me coming to you."

James literally saw red for a moment, but it wasn't until Wendy put a hand on his forearm then he managed to regain control of his anger and breathe deeply before answering. "How about this? Unload your ship, put all the treasure on mine, and fly away while you still can. According to Mr. Smee's reading of the planet, there's a nice lava flow just a few miles from here. I'd be happy to drop you in there and warm you up if you don't agree to my current terms."

He reached over to take Wendy's hand, and she didn't resist. In fact, she melted against him when he put his arm around her. "And so we're clear, Pan, Wendy's going nowhere with you. She belongs with me."

"With, not to," said Wendy from the side of her mouth in a whisper. She appeared to approve of his word choice, and she winked at him.

"I told you," said Tink with a crow of

laughter. "She's a slut. Your precious Wendy went from your bed to someone else's in days."

Hook turned his rifle toward Tink at the insult, but she appeared oblivious. She was more focused on Wendy, who suddenly took a running start at her and knocked her to the ground. It seemed to be the unspoken signal, and Pan's crew tried to run away. James wasn't surprised that it had escalated, and he certainly wasn't disappointed as he approached Pan while nodding at his people to fan out and intercept the others.

The battle was vicious, but over quickly. James was unable to monitor most of it as he kept his attention on Pan, with his pathetic sword. This time, he just dodged out of the way since Turley was too far for James to borrow his. Soon enough, he had Peter Pan pinned to the ground with his rifle against his chin, sitting casually on his chest as the others rounded up the rest of the crew.

Except Wendy. He frowned as he

looked around, not seeing her or Tink anywhere. "What happened to Wendy?"

"The Faetian got away from her, but she was running after her last I saw," said Cookson.

James cursed. "Spread out and find her as soon as we have the others secure."

He stood up, reluctantly tying up Pan as well, despite his plan to just sit on him, literally, while his crew retrieved the treasure from the *Pixie Dust* and loaded it onto the *Jolly Roger*.

They set out in less than five minutes, though James left two of his men behind act as guards for the tied-up crew of the *Pixie Dust*. The planet, since it lacked vegetation, was easy enough to traverse, and he could see Wendy ahead. She was clearly frustrated as she turned to meet him when he approached. "The bitch slipped away from me, and then she just disappeared. I don't know how she did it. I could hear her voice for a bit, but couldn't pinpoint its location, since she kept moving."

"It was likely some kind of camouflage device," said Smee. "That means she has to be around here somewhere."

Wendy nodded. "I saw footprints for a while, but then the wind started blowing, and the sand quickly covered them again. The wind also made it impossible to tell whom she called, but I'll bet it wasn't anyone we want to see."

"Everyone stand in line behind me," said James. He pitched his voice loudly enough so Tink could hear if she was anywhere in the vicinity. "I'm going to fire randomly, and we'll know if we hit her, because she'll bleed, with or without camouflage. She can't hide once blood drops hit the ground.

"Wait," called Tink's irritating voice. She flickered into view a moment later with her hands in the air. "Don't shoot me." She seemed to be going for vulnerable and frightened, but the smirk on her face ruined that effect.

Wendy glared at her before looking at James and shaking her head. "She's up to something. You can tell from her expression, and it's probably not good for us. We should get out of here as fast as we can."

"I agree." He turned back to Tink. "Remove the camo-emitter and toss it this way, before walking slowly toward us."

She made a production of it, going as slowly as possible, but was finally near them with her fingers twined and hands behind her head as she stood before them.

"On your knees."

Tink glared at him. "Don't get any funny ideas, Hook. There's only one man I get on my knees for."

Wendy made a gagging sound as James shuddered. "Feel free not to share his name." He was certain it would be Peter Pan, but he didn't need the confirmation strengthening the unpleasant visual he was already having trouble escaping.

Once Wendy had tied Tink, perhaps a little tighter than necessary, Turley and

Bott picked her up to drag between them back to the area where they had left the rest of Pan's crew under guard. They found them in much the same way, and James quickly ordered the rest of his crew to start loading the treasure from the *Pixie Dust* onto the *Jolly Roger*.

When they finished that, they turned their attention to the pit in the ground, and it was still bulging with platinum bars. Pan's crew had apparently chosen to focus on the rhodium bars, since they were worth more, but now James's crew would have all of both.

No sooner had he the thought than there was a booming sound less than a kilometer from them. "What was that?"

"It appears to be a ship, Captain," said Ceeco after looking at a handheld device. "We didn't see it sooner because it was camouflaged."

"Croc," said James. It was more of a declaration than a question, and he didn't actually need confirmation. "Finish loading what you can, and let's get out of here."

"But the pit's still half-full," said Smee.

James shrugged. "We have plenty to finance our new life, so let's go." He thought they might make it as they hustled toward the *Jolly Roger* a minute later, but drew to a halt a few feet away as Croc and his crew fanned out to face them.

Croc must've had at least fifty Karolilans, all in Coalition uniforms, with him, and James's crew of nine was badly outnumbered. Crew of ten if he counted Wendy, but he didn't know how much actual fighting experience she had, at least when facing a Karolilan instead of a Faetian who was almost the same size as her.

"No survivors," shouted Croc in a hoarse, hissy voice. The reptilian-like features of his race were enough to send a shiver down James's spine despite having seen him a number of times. He couldn't help recalling how Tikta had eaten the few times he'd been invited to share a meal with the admiral. He consumed uncooked flesh, and he wasn't terribly picky about whether or not the source was still alive or dead. James's stomach quivered when he remembered the time Croc had munched on live *bellons* from Crepitus, which vaguely resembled Earth lobster, though quite a bit larger.

The Karolilans were a vicious race, and being given carte blanch to destroy James's crew was chilling. "Defend yourselves to the last man," said James. With that, they were surrounded and focused on fighting their way out. They had to spread out to engage, and also to avoid shooting each other or being shot, but he tried to keep track of his crewmates as they fought, and especially Wendy.

He lost track of her as he faced off with one of Croc's commanders, eventually landing a shot between the creature's close-set eyes that dropped it to the ground of the desolate planet with a stirring of sand. That gave him a small breather, and he was able to find Wendy. A surge of cold anger went through him when he saw her struggling with Tink, who held a gun to her head. Wendy was still fighting despite Tink's insistence to stop, and James rushed toward them. He pointed his gun at Tink. "Free Wendy."

"I'm going to kill her." Tink pressed the gun viciously into Wendy's temple, making her whimper.

"If you even think about pulling the trigger, I'll shoot you." James lined up his target, centering on the thumping of Tink's heart with his thermal site. "I can end you."

"Do it," said Wendy. He'd never seen her so angry, or so beautiful. She reminded him of a vengeful Valkyrie, and he was certain that she would tear Tink apart if she could get the opening to do so.

"I'm afraid I'll shoot you if I try to shoot her, love," said James. His tone hardened when he looked at Tink again. "But I'll take the chance if I must."

"Release the girl," said Croc across the way from James. His gun was pointed at James, but James didn't move his targeting from Tink.

Tink looked confused. "I'm the one who called you."

"I assumed, since it had to be you or the human female, but she appears to be on Hook's side. Let go of her now, retrieve what you can carry of the treasure, and take the shuttle that's waiting for you by my ship, as agreed. Then clear out of the area."

"Wait! I need to take Peter with me."

Croc looked angry, though James found it difficult to tell when his default expression was always moderately annoyed. "That wasn't part of the negotiation."

"Please." Tink seemed to be on the verge of tears.

Croc shrugged. "You're both wanted criminals, and I'll catch up with you later, but enjoy your brief taste of freedom with

Pan."

Tink scrambled up, and Wendy kicked out at her as she got to her feet. James laughed at the gesture, feeling insanely proud of his woman, even though she missed aside from a glancing blow off Tink's calf that barely slowed down the Faetian woman.

Unfortunately, the kick delayed Wendy to the point she couldn't escape Croc, who reached her first and just seconds before James. He aimed his gun at Croc instead, and his finger hovered on the trigger. If it hadn't been for Croc taking the cowardly action of holding Wendy in front of him to shield the bulk of his frame, James would've done away with his nemesis right then. "Release her."

"I'll be in touch, Hook. You know what I want, and you'll bring it to the designated meeting spot, or your human female will be fed to my starfish, whole and alive."

James shuddered, recalling the large tank in the bar where he'd tracked Croc that housed the bioluminescent, glowing fish he'd collected from an unknown planet. The way they glowed and twinkled in the dark led to their idyllic name, since they resembled stars, but there was nothing else pleasant about them. They were voracious carnivores and had stripped the flesh from his severed hand in seconds when Croc tossed it into their tank that long-ago night he'd gone for revenge and ended up with a prosthetic hand. "If you harm her at all, I'll make you suffer before I kill you."

"But if I don't harm her, you'll turn over the evidence and the device, and allow me to live?" The admiral spoke with clear skepticism.

"No, of course not. I'll likely kill you either way, but I'll make sure you feel every moment if you hurt her. Otherwise, I'm inclined to deal with you quickly to get you out of my life once and for all."

Croc laughed, clearly disbelieving as he clamped Wendy tighter to him. "Remember to show up at the coordinates I'm going to send, and perhaps you'll get your smelly human back in one piece." He started dragging Wendy away.

James rushed forward, trying to reach her, but Croc's men surrounded him. There was no way to her without giving one of them the opening to kill him as he tried to run after Wendy. If he died now, there would be no rescuing her from Croc later.

That didn't stop him from trying to fight his way through the remaining thirty or so of Croc's crew, but by the time he and the other eight men on his crew had managed to subdue all of them, they could hear *The Bogey* taking off in the distance. James cursed long and low as Smee came to him, placing a hand on his shoulder.

"We'll get her back, James."

James nodded. Perhaps he appeared stoic, but the truth was, if he opened his mouth, he was either going to scream or howl with grief and fury that Croc had taken Wendy. To keep it together, he had to remain quiet until he could regain control.

"About the evidence and the dematerializer...?" Smee trailed off for a moment. "Are you really going to hand them over, Captain?"

James wanted to say no. He'd refused to allow such a dangerous weapon to fall into Croc's or the Coalition's hands until now, but keeping them from the technology no longer seemed that important. His universe had distilled down to Wendy, and he could no longer protect anyone else, including his father, if it meant leaving Wendy in Croc's hands.

Chapter Eleven

The slimy, scaly admiral didn't release her until they had boarded his ship, and the door sealed behind them. Then he shoved her a few feet away from him and sniffed deeply. His nostrils flared, and a forked tongue extended from his mouth. "Why do you humans always smell so foul? Your stench caused us to prolong the war an additional decade just to avoid having to work closely with you."

She didn't bother to answer, since she found his musty aroma equally objectionable. She glared at him while warily eyeing the remaining crew that surrounded them as they reentered the ship. For the fifty he'd brought with him to the surface, there must be another twenty-five on board, and that likely didn't include those who were manning vital stations right then. *The Bogey* was twice the size of the *Jolly Roger*, but she would bet the *Jolly Roger* was still faster. The disparity in James's crew size versus Croc's worried her though.

"Why are you glaring at me, human? I just rescued you from the most notorious space pirate in Coalition territory."

"I don't particularly like Karolilans," she said with angry inflection.

His wide mouth opened, revealing sharp teeth. "Why is that? You've heard the rumors that Karolilans eat humans? We haven't consumed human flesh since we signed a treaty with the Coalition years ago. And before that, you were never a favorite meal for any of us, due to the lingering stench."

"Your kind killed my parents, who were innocent terraformers working for the Coalition. We didn't even have weapons at the TF colony."

He laughed. "You're going to have to be more specific, human."

Wendy tensed, feeling the urge to throw herself at him and try to scratch out his eyes. Fortunately, common sense and self-preservation kicked in to prevent her from following the reckless compulsion. "A28Z."

One of his eyes became larger than the other. He didn't have eyebrows, so she couldn't say that he arched a brow, but he definitely had a look of puzzlement. "And what is A28Z?"

"The planet your people destroyed fourteen standardized Coalition rotations ago. Samuel and Blair Darling died that day, along with one hundred and thirty-two other terraformers and their families. Two hundred and thirty-eight people managed to escape, but of those, only one hundred and eighty-four survived after your people started shooting down life pods." She might have been just twelve at the time, but she could remember it all as clearly as though it had happened just yesterday.

He frowned for a moment and then nodded. "Yes, that was the planet we called Besenor. It was clearly ours, and we had to defend it. It was interesting that our treaty survived the eviction of Coalition people from our territory, but not terribly surprising. Most humans are cowards and didn't want to resume hostilities after a generation of peace."

"A28Z was disputed territory and fell under treaty guidelines. The Karolilans should have given people a chance to evacuate without shooting them."

"Sadly, I wasn't there, but I'm sure Karolilan forces followed the established procedure for such a situation. Truly, it's of no consequence to me, though I must admit it would be a delicious irony if I had been one involved in dispatching your family. That wasn't the case." He seemed genuinely mournful about that.

Wendy couldn't control the impulse any longer. Hearing him admit he was sorry not to have been involved in killing her parents made her lose all sense of control for a moment, and she launched herself at him. She almost reached him before his crew intercepted her, catching and dragging her backward to shove her to the floor. They handled her more roughly than they needed to, and her shoulder collided with the steel floor of the ship, but she refused to cry out and give them any satisfaction.

A second later, Croc's foot rested on her head, pressing her deeper into the metal. He outweighed her by at least a hundred pounds, and since it was all compact muscle underneath his scaly skin, she doubted he would have little trouble crushing her skull. She should be frightened, but all she could feel was the rage still burning through her. "You're going to die," she said through her compressed lips, which were smashed into the steel floor on one side of her mouth.

"You're an amusing little thing, human female. Perhaps I have a glimmer of what Hook sees in you, but I could never get past your unpleasant stench and fleshiness. Lucky for you, I need you." He lifted his foot off her head and took a step back. "Take her to the brig and leave her there until I call for her. We need her for the exchange, and then it doesn't matter what happens to her. In the meantime, ensure she survives." He paused and turned back to give her a cold smile. "But allow her to see the starfish eating before you do so." He looked at Wendy again. "You'll be their next meal if you fail to cooperate."

Wendy struggled to be stoic as they lifted her off the floor and then completely off her feet. The two guards carrying her were larger and taller than her, and they seemed to have little difficulty with the task. She didn't struggle, deciding to save her energy for an escape attempt.

They moved through a few corridors before reaching an access door that was clearly more secured than others. Wendy's stomach churned as they stepped inside, and it took a moment to absorb they were in almost perfect darkness, except for pinpricks of light surrounding them.

"Must be hungry," said the guard on her left with a grunt. "They're dull tonight. Mustn't have eaten for a few days."

The other one grunted a response before pressing a button with his elbow. Neither of them released their hold on Wendy.

A second later, a large splashing sound coincided with a sudden increase in the brightness. In seconds, the pinpricks of light became glowing balls that provided enough illumination for her to see how quickly—and viciously—they devoured whatever lifeform had been dropped in their tank, still alive. She shuddered and turned her head.

"Nasty little buggers, aren't they?" asked one of her guards with a chuckle. "The admiral finds them charming, so he insists on taking them wherever he goes. They've proven quite *handy* in the past." He chortled.

"Real *handy*," said the other guard. "Just ask Hook."

Their implication sank in as they dragged her from the starfish room to another room down the corridor, which revealed cells, and she recalled James telling her Croc had planned to cut him up and feed him to his fish. A similar fate awaited her, and she doubted any amount of cooperation could buy her way out of that.

She braced herself when they reached an empty cell, knowing they were going to throw her in before they even let go. They did as she expected, and she tried to roll herself into a ball with her arms over her head to protect it. Her elbow slammed into one of the walls, but that was the worst of the impact.

It was bad enough to make her arm vibrate with pain and have her curl up as she breathed through the agony, until it faded from a sharp pulsing hurt to a dull, throbbing ache a few moments later.

At that point, she set up, and her gaze locked with a pair of green eyes opposite her. She couldn't keep her lip curling upward when she recognized Tink. "Just when I thought it couldn't be any worse than to be locked in his brig near his insane fish, I find I have to share the space with you."

"Are you all right?" asked Peter.

"Fine."

"You can't trust Croc. He double-crossed me and Tink."

"I guess you and he have that in common," said Wendy as she laid her face against her knees and tried to ignore them. At least they were in the cell next to her, so she wasn't in touching range, and neither were they. Unhappily, that meant she probably wouldn't get a chance to strangle Tink before they were removed from the brig.

"I don't know what you're talking about," said Peter with a good imitation of indignation.

"Save your breath and your lies, Pan. James told me everything about what you did to him. I always knew you were a man of questionable ethics, but didn't expect you to be the type to attack a partner with his back turned toward you. Although, in retrospect, it doesn't seem all that surprising." How could she have ever mistaken Peter for a bad boy when he was just a bad person?

"He has no right to do this," said Tink. "When I contacted Croc, he promised me safe passage, a share of the treasure, and your captivity. He's a liar."

"Yes, he is." Wendy chuckled again.

"Why are you so happy?" asked Tink in an angry voice. "You're his prisoner too."

"Yes, but I have someone coming to

rescue me. I doubt you two cutthroats have any friends or allies left in the galaxy who would bother to risk their neck to save you."

Peter frowned. "Who's going to save you?"

"James will."

Peter crossed his arms over his chest. "I don't like you spending time with James Hook. You've changed, Wendy."

Wendy almost laughed, but didn't quite have the energy. "I guess I've changed a little, or at least I've stopped being so naïve. I can see exactly what kind of person you are now, and if I'd realized it months ago, I never would've wasted my time leaving New London to be with you." Despite her words, she couldn't regret her actions. They'd brought her into James's sphere, and she might never have met her scalawag pirate captain otherwise.

And he felt completely like hers, a fact she needed to tell him once they were reunited.

"She slept with him, Peter. Don't you

understand? I warned you she would, didn't I?" Tink was practically bouncing up and down in her joy.

"You warned me she would probably sleep with Kubrick and all me other mates. You didn't say anything about James Hook."

Peter's petulant voice was irritating enough to set Wendy's teeth on edge. "I did sleep with him, and I enjoyed every moment of it. Multiple times. Sometimes multiple times in the same night." She chortled at Peter's look of outrage, but really lost it when she saw Tink's faintly envious expression. "As I'm sure you're aware, that never happened with Peter." She giggled madly to herself, managing to block out their protests and further words.

Once she regained control of her mirth, Wendy got off the floor of the cell and moved over to the metal bunk that apparently did double duty as a bed. She stretched across it and turned away from them, finding it to be the most uncomfortable place she'd ever slept, and only partly because the metal bunk didn't yield at all. Being forced to share this confined space with Tink and Peter surely counted as some kind of violation of the ethical code for the treatment of prisoners.

1

©WENDY thought it had only been a couple of days, though it felt more like ten years being trapped with those two as they bickered with each other and tried to draw her in on it, before *The Bogey* dropped out of ionospace and clearly started its descent toward landing.

"What's going on?" called Peter. Over the last two days, he hadn't seemed to realize that either no one was monitoring the cells to listen when he spoke, or they just didn't care when he talked, because none of them had responded yet.

Since they'd remained out of sight, other than to bring one meal and a jug of water per day, it was a surprise to see two of the Karolilans and a small group of humans in Coalition uniforms appear a few moments later, as though Peter's question had summoned them. Wendy stood up, bracing herself as she eyed the Coalition forces, who wore the same uniform as Croc's people, but somehow looked different.

Perhaps it was just the way the Karolilans had to tailor their Coalition uniforms to fit their odd shape compared to humans. Whatever it was, she could definitely see a clear delineation between them and was positive the humans following the Karolilans weren't part of Croc's crew.

"Peter Pan and Tink Rabelle, you're both wanted criminals in multiple sectors of Coalition territory. There're also five extradition requests for you from territories not yet under Coalition control. You're under arrest for piracy, robbery, and vandalism of Coalition property." Those words came from a rough older man. His uniform was perfectly tidy, but something about himself seemed slovenly. "How do you plead?"

"We aren't pleading to anything until we talk to a representative," said Tink.

"Not guilty," said Peter at the same time.

"Ask for representation, you idiot," said Tink. She rolled her eyes. "If you don't, you'll disappear into their prison system as they wait to process you with the other Not Guiltys. You could be there for years."

Peter started sweating. "Yeah, okay. What she said. I want representation."

The slovenly officer looked almost disappointed at their answer. "In that case, you'll be processed to await representation. There's currently a backlog of eight months, and you'll be held as a prisoner until you have a chance to consult with a representative and enter your plea. Take them away."

Wendy braced herself as the guards removed Tink and Peter from the cell they had shared, waiting for them to turn their attention to her. She was thankful Tink had shared information about requesting a representative, because Wendy had never been arrested and had never even looked into the procedure. Eight months to receive a representative seemed obscene, but it sounded better than years waiting for a Not Guilty trial.

To her surprise, they completely ignored her as they hustled Tink and Peter out of the brig. She waited until the Coalition humans had cleared the area before asking the nearest Karolilan, who was just about to leave, "What about me?"

"You have other value to the admiral," said the man in a rough voice, and the laugh he issued afterward did nothing to soften his appearance of cruel strength.

When they returned to ionospace a short time later, she was happy to have some peace and quiet. It was more pleasant to be in prison now that she didn't have Peter and Tink constantly filling the background with noise, but certainly not enjoyable. She was confident

James would come for her, and she just had to wait.

1

WENDY had a difficult time judging the time, but was certain it hadn't even been a day before the ship dropped out of ionospace again and slowed its speed to descend into an atmosphere. There were no windows around her, but she could feel the ship setting down a short time later, so she stiffened. She was preparing herself for any manner of unpleasantries when the two guards came to fetch her, and she walked between them.

To her surprise, they didn't bother to bind her hands, and she wasn't certain if that was because they considered her no threat at all, or because they were trying to placate James into believing she'd been treated well to catch him off-guard. Even though she had been reasonably well-treated, other than having to endure Peter and Tink, she still didn't their goal was to signal that.

She was slightly confused by their actions, but walked along with them as they led her off the ship. She stumbled to a halt when her feet touched muddy ground beneath her. They were in an area that looked like a swamp, and each step they took made squelching sounds. She quickly got over her disgust with the terrain when she looked up and saw the crew of the *Jolly Roger* fanned out nearby.

But where was James? She didn't see him anywhere. For a moment, she almost fell to her knees as the reality hit her. He must have been killed in the battle with Croc's remaining men. That was the only thing that would've kept him from being there, and she was sure of that.

"Where is Hook?" thundered Tikta Croc. He was glaring at the crew of the *Jolly Roger* while shouting the question.

"Right here," said James softly from behind them.

Croc spun quickly, and Wendy managed to wrench away from her guards enough to do the same. She let out a small sob of relief when she saw James standing behind her, and though she couldn't get to him, she was suddenly far more optimistic about how this was going to end.

"How did you get back there? There was no sign of you a moment ago."

"Dematerialization." James picked up a device that looked roughly the size of a small trunk and had a strap to make it easier to cross-carry over his body. "It's only a portable prototype, but my people," His gaze strayed toward Ceeco for a minute, "Managed to succeed where the kKloptins failed. It's a working prototype, and it's yours as soon as you release Wendy."

Croc looked pleased, but made no move to release Wendy. Instead, he took a step toward James. "And the recording?"

"What if I told you I destroyed the recording long ago to protect my...him?" asked James without blinking.

Croc shook his head. "Oh, Hook, do you

really think I'm going to fall for that? While it implicates a certain someone, it also somewhat exonerates you and proves you had nothing to do with dispatching the Kloptins. I would suspect that my revelation of who was the head of our black-ops sector is what's kept you from sharing it all this time and removing your Coalition warrant."

Wendy grew alarmed when James paled and swayed slightly before his shoulders stiffened. Whatever Croc was saying, it must've hit James hard.

"You're correct, but I can no longer hide my father's involvement in the black-ops missions you undertake. The last I heard, he's old and feeble, so he'll likely face little punishment for what he's done. It's not my concern any longer, and I suppose it hasn't been mine since he turned his back on me and agreed to let you convince the Coalition I was the one guilty for your crimes."

"That was a stroke of genius on the old man's part," said Croc with a thick chuckle. "It certainly lent credence to my story when your own father refused to view the footage and announced he believed my version of events. Of course, he would do that, wouldn't he? He had too much to lose to support you. Now, hand over the footage."

James extracted something small that he passed to one the guards standing near him. That Karolilan ferried it over to Croc. "Thank you, Bick." The admiral slipped it into a handheld scanner to watch the footage contained within. The scanner projected it as a 3D life-size image.

Wendy could only watch a little of it as Croc and his men undertook the wholesale slaughter of people who were already injured, often pleading for their lives, and clearly in no position to fight back any longer. Near the end of the footage, James asked Croc why he was doing this, since it was contrary to Coalition guidelines, and Croc told him what their mission was. When he mentioned Bartholomew Hook was the head of his division, a much younger James swayed and looked away.

After that, James and his crew lingered on the sidelines, silently observing and recording, but not interceding or speaking again. A small sound from him made Wendy look at James, and she saw the guilt on James's face as he watched the old footage intently. Though he must've seen it before, he seemed unusually focused on it—especially with the cybernetic eye. That thought sent a jolt of excitement through her. She wasn't certain what he was doing, but his intensity seemed to indicate there was a plan in motion.

"Excellent." Croc ejected the small disk and dropped it into the muck before stomping on it with his booted foot. Mud flew around from his agitating motion, and when he lifted his foot a moment later, the disk was in shards. "I want a demonstration of the dematerializer.

James cocked a brow. "I'm surprised

you're brave enough to try it, Croc."

"I doubt you'll try to cross me when I have your woman. Bick, point your gun at her forehead, and if Hook so much as sneezes, shoot her."

"Yes, sir," said the one identified as Bick.

He was one of the two guards she'd seen intermittently over the last few days, but she still had no idea what the other one's name was, and she didn't care. Wendy struggled to remain calm when Bick's pistol pressed against her forehead, and she looked away from it to maintain eye contact with James, striving to project her confidence in him across the distance separating them.

Croc approached slowly, and James made no move to lift a weapon. All he did was press a button, and the device admitted a light that seemed to scan Croc. There was a humming sound, and then a moment later, Croc disappeared. He reappeared on the other side of Wendy and Bick, having taken a journey of no more than five feet, but it was clearly enough to convince him. "Excellent, it does work. You've been most useful, Hook."

James nodded at Croc's exclamation. "Release Wendy. You have what you wanted, so let us go."

Croc shook his head. "And here I thought you were less naïve after years of reality, Hook. How do I know you gave me the only copy of the recording? And how can I turn you over to Coalition prisons for justice? You might crack, and someone might eventually believe you. No, it's a risk I can't take, so you'll all have to die."

"I can assure you, Admiral Croc, that the footage is the only copy, but that doesn't mean you're the only one to see it. I've broadcast it to all the planets in range, and I've already uploaded it to the Coalition computers and sent it to President Varga. I have a feeling the Coalition leader will have some hard questions for you, as will most of the rest of the galaxy."

It was Croc's turn to pale, which made him a gray-green color, and he swallowed thickly. "You're lying."

James grinned. "Afraid not. If you'd just let me go, I would've taken the blame for your crimes to protect my father. It would've been worth it to keep the technology that many in the Coalition will try to misuse out of your hands. When you involved Wendy, the woman I love, you made the biggest mistake of your life, Croc, and with any luck, one of the last. If I'm not mistaken, the death penalty is still on the books for treason, and it's one of the few times it's ever used. I sincerely hope I live long enough to see you face the consequences of your actions."

"You double-crossing—" Croc lunged toward James, but disappeared with a humming sound and flash of light.

Wendy was stunned for a moment, but not as stunned as her guard. She took advantage of his distraction to bend down and slam her fist into his groin. Bick fell to the ground, cradling his testicles and rolling around as the other guard who'd watched over her the past few days came running toward her.

Wendy dropped the rest of the way to the ground and rolled out of his path, getting to her feet and running to James before the guard could catch her. James lifted his pistol, and she saw the laser discharge. Wendy darted to the right to avoid it, and there was a groan behind her, followed by a solid-sounding thud that indicated the guard had hit the ground heavily.

The rest of Croc's men stood around, and they all appeared lost. She could imagine they were trying to decide what was the best course of action—try to escape before the Coalition came, plausible deniability, or simply execute Hook and the rest of his crew, and try to suppress the evidence.

She was certain that would be the path least likely to work, and not just because the crew was determined to avoid being caught. They couldn't delete the footage

James had broadcast to the galaxy, so their odds of suppressing any evidence were infinitesimal—though she didn't know if they were smart enough to grasp that. Maybe she was giving them too much credit, and they were still trying to figure out where Croc was.

She looked around. "Where's the admiral?"

"When the device scanned him, it stored his genetic profile. As long as he's within range, it can transport him. It's one of the convenience features, though I doubt he finds it particularly convenient." James had a huge grin on his face. He picked up the device, and his cybernetic eye focused on the control panel. "Croc is currently in a holding pattern, and he can be released to whatever coordinates you choose by inputting them and pressing this red button." He seemed to be speaking in an impersonal way to any official who might be viewing the moment. After that, he set down the dematerializer and appeared less intense.

"And consider yourself lucky I don't drop the Twins on you, Croc," he said in a softer voice.

Wendy thought that meant he had stopped recording. She threw herself into his arms, relishing in the feel of them around her. She couldn't resist pressing kisses to his face as he swept her into his arms while the crew of the *Jolly Roger* surrounded them. She forced herself to break away from the kiss long enough to ask, "What are the twins?"

James shook his head. "It doesn't matter. I consider it lucky that we didn't need them and hope we never will. If this lot doesn't resist, we won't, anyway." He looked to where Croc's men had been.

Apparently, Croc's crewmembers had chosen not to try to apprehend them. The Karolilans currently scurried to *The Bogey* like their tails were on fire, clearly having decided to try their luck at running. She didn't care enough to try to stop them, since Croc was captured.

Instead, she turned back to James and

kissed him fully on the mouth. It was a passionate joining of their lips, since it felt like they'd been separated for years instead of days. "I knew you'd come for me," she said when she pulled back.

"I tried to come sooner," said James at the same time. He grinned when she did before adding, "We had to wait for Croc to contact us with the coordinates, but there was never a doubt I was going to come after you."

She frowned as she remembered what the footage had revealed. "Is it true? Is your father involved in all this?"

James looked sad. "Yes, it's true. At first, I didn't believe Croc when he told me, but then my father turned his back on me and said I was dishonorable. When I finally escaped and had my brain working again after Smee and Ceeco got me out of the confrontation with Croc, I did some digging. It wasn't that hard to confirm, though it shocked me, because he'd told me all about the Hook honor from the time I was a little boy."

"Why didn't you say something sooner? Or let the world know you were innocent?" asked Wendy. "You wouldn't have had to run from Croc all these years."

James shrugged. "I was trying to shield my siblings, though they all wrote me off like he did. Part of my actions were to protect my father as well. He's a man deeply committed to his ideals. He probably thinks this black-ops nonsense is the right thing, and he's doing important work. I would've been content to be the scapegoat if Croc hadn't dragged you into it."

"I'm glad he did, because you deserve to be exonerated."

James chuckled then. "Oh, love, you don't think I'm going to be pardoned, do you? Obviously, they can't keep charging me for treason any longer with the public broadcast to this part of the galaxy, but I'm still a wanted man on many other planets, and I'm certainly far more for pirate than Coalition captain these days.

There's no easy pardon for us, I'm afraid. The most we can do is take our vast fortune and find a quiet planet on which to settle, which is the plan."

"You're not going to be a pirate anymore?" Wendy couldn't fathom the idea. There was still so much of the bad boy about her lover that it seemed impossible to imagine him living some idyllic life on a backwater planet.

"No, it isn't safe. It's time we settled down and behaved responsibly."

Wendy started to protest, but decided not to. Time would tell if James could truly settle into such a lifestyle, or if his own urges would get the better of him. She found herself hoping her bad boy pirate was still in there, but it didn't matter either way. She loved James Hook regardless of which path he took. Which reminded her... "Did you mean it?"

He cocked a brow as he put his arm around her waist, gently guiding her toward the gangplank of the *Jolly Roger*. "Mean what?"

"That you loved me? You called me the woman you loved."

His eyes sparkled. "That's because you are the woman I love, Wendy. No past tense about it. You should know that I've decided to claim you, and you're the best treasure I've ever found. No one will be prying you away from me."

"And if I wish to be pried away?" She had no such desire, but she couldn't help probing.

"Not even you can make me let you leave, Wendy. We belong together." Some of his arrogant confidence faded, and vulnerability shown through in both his human and cybernetic eyes. "Don't you feel the connection between us? Or have I imagined something?"

She shook her head. "No, you haven't imagined anything. I love you too, James. I'll go with you wherever you go, but I'm not promising to follow your every command except maybe when I'm a crewmate." She knew enough about how his mind worked to add that qualifier at the end.

"Perhaps someday you'll come to my way of thinking and learn to enjoy accepting my commands." As he said the words, he bent his head to kiss her, and there was no doubting or denying the passion he displayed.

Wendy wasn't surprised when he hustled her straight to his quarters instead of the bridge, and he didn't even bother to designate Smee or Ceeco as having command for the moment. No one seemed to mind the lapse of command etiquette, and she couldn't be bothered to focus on it as James closed the door behind them, and they lost themselves in each other's arms.

ℰPILOGUE

Five months later

𝔍AMES had settled into the quiet life better than Wendy had anticipated, but it was obvious after just a few months that he was growing antsy. He hadn't said anything, and neither had she, but she was looking for an adventure as well. As lovely as their paradise planet was, especially since it was out of Coalition control and well off the route that would place it at risk for Coalition expansion for at least the next century, she was bored and restless as well.

Yet they had no reason to steal or commit crimes, so they were at an impasse. It was Wendy who first suggested he could still work against the Coalition while doing good. She got the idea from seeing a Coalition report on the trade embargo imposed on a non-Coalition-affiliated planet. It was one planet against the entire Coalition, and they were keeping food and medicine from crossing supply lines. Wendy showed James the broadcast, and she could see the moment when he had the same idea she did by the way his eyes sparkled, and he grinned at her.

"It could be dangerous," he'd said.

"I live for danger." She'd laughed as she said those words across the breakfast table. "And we'd be doing something useful. Those people need food and medicine, whether or not their leaders refuse to join the Coalition. The Coalition has no right to do deny their people necessities."

"And the Gerrians will be stubborn about it. I can't blame them for not wanting to kowtow and join the Coalition, but from what I know of their species, they'll fight to the end rather than surrender. All those people will suffer in the meantime." James was frowning. "It just doesn't seem right, does it?"

Wendy shook her head. "No, it doesn't. I think we should sneak in food and medicine to them. The *Jolly Roger*, er, the *Unity*, is up for the trip now that she has a new designation and paint job."

"I don't believe I'll ever adjust to calling the *Jolly Roger* anything but her name, but *Unity* is certainly ready to fly. I don't think it'd take much to interest the old crew, at least those living on our planet or in the vicinity. With Cecco back home at his family's, he's probably out, but..."

Their conversation had turned to practical matters, along with planning, and how they could acquire what they needed and slip through the blockade. They'd started the planning stage two weeks ago, and now they were at the rendezvous point. While Ceeco hadn't been interested in their humanitarian mission, he'd proven invaluable with establishing communications with the leader of the Gerrians, and now they were meeting on Gerra to drop off much-needed supplies.

Kimbrough, who was the leader of the Gerrians, still seemed shocked that they had actually delivered. "We can't pay you," he said again for the third time.

"No payment is necessary," said James, Wendy beamed at him. "We're doing this because it's the right thing to do, and because it thwarts the Coalition." He chuckled. "I like that. It's a perk."

The leader shrugged. "In that case, we thank you. The Gerrians owe you a blood debt, so if you ever need to collect it, please don't hesitate to do so." Kimbrough extended his hand, and James took it. It was an awkward, sideways handshake, and Wendy focused on it so she could repeat the motion when it was her turn.

A moment later, the leader repeated the hand shake with her before turning to direct his people to load the cargo on the fleet of trucks awaiting. He lifted his fist as they walked away, but didn't look back.

Wendy and James were soon back aboard the *Jolly Roger*, er, *Unity*. Hand-in-hand they headed toward the bridge, though she would've liked to divert to their quarters. There was no time for that, at least until they were safely through the blockade again, but Briar, their new navigations officer, seemed well up to the task, and with the camouflage upgrades from Juud and Andony Ceeco, the *Unity* sailed through as though invisible to the Coalition.

Sometime later, they dropped out of ionospace, and Smee tuned in the Coalition news channels. They were all listening for some information about the drop they'd made to Gerra, wondering if they'd been detected. Instead, they were greeted with a breaking news story of Coalition forces invading Necto's planet to arrest him. They finally had enough evidence to indict him for crimes against the Coalition.

"Tax evasion," said James with a shake of his head.

Wendy nodded. It hardly seemed fair that he would go down for tax evasion, but at least he was going down. She hadn't really thought of him since that brief time she'd been involved in James's mission, and they disappeared too quickly for Necto to extract revenge, but he would probably have come after them at some point. Having him in prison was one less worry on her mind. Not that Necto had occupied much space in her mind anyway. He hardly seemed like a match for her wily and roguish pirate captain.

"Captain Hook?" Wendy used a sweet tone.

He looked away from the vid screen.

"Yes, Ensign Darling. ""

"I need to discuss a training manual with you. In private."

James's eyes widened, and he clearly understood where she was going with that invitation. He nodded and cleared his throat. "Mr. Smee, you have the bridge until I return."

"Aye, Captain," said Smee with a knowing chuckle.

Wendy took James's hand as they walked down the corridor to their shared quarters, basking in the connection between them. Once the door closed behind her, she was startled when James turned and pressed her against it. "Captain, whatever are you doing?"

"Down there on the planet, I told you to stay behind me while we approached Kimbrough, in case he had a trap in mind. Instead, you stepped in front of me and made yourself vulnerable while contravening my direct order."

She blinked innocently. "I don't remember you saying that."

"Liar," he said with a chuckle before leaning forward to give her a punishing kiss. "You deliberately disobeyed, Ensign Darling."

She tilted her head to the side, trying to decide how to play it before nodding. "Yes, I absolutely did, Captain Hook. Are you going to punish me now?" Her bottom grew warm just at the thought, and she couldn't hold back a moan of anticipation. Over the last few months, she'd discovered a fondness for James's unique methods of discipline, especially when they involved his hand warming her ass.

"I certainly am." He pulled her over to the bed, sitting down before dragging her across his lap. Wendy offered a token protest she wasn't really feeling, and he clearly knew that. A moment later, his hand slammed down on her butt, and it was nice enough to make her wriggle, but lacked true heat because she still wore pants.

Ever the perceptive captain, James

quickly stripped down her pants to reveal her bare bottom before turning it a toasty pink while she wriggled against his lap and moaned under his punishment.

As nice as the punishment was, it was the aftercare that she really craved. He laid her back on the bed a short time later, parting her thighs so his tongue could slip inside her pussy. Wendy moaned and arched against him as he licked her clit before sucking on it. "I love you, James," she shouted as an orgasm swept over her moments later. There was no pretense of Captain and Ensign at the moment. They were simply James and Wendy, two lovers in love, and there was no reason to hide her love or desire.

James was eager for her, and she could tell by the way he fumbled with his pants only long enough to free his shaft before pressing their bodies together as one. They thrust together in harmony, maintaining a synchronized pace, as she spiraled closer to another release. James was only a second behind her, filling her insides a few moments later with proof of his satisfaction as it mingled with hers.

Afterward, she laid against him, exhausted, and he pressed a kiss to her forehead. "I love you too, Wendy, and I think the *Jolly Roger* isn't the only one due for a name change."

She shifted slightly to look up at him, allowing her confusion to show. "I'm not sure what you mean, James."

"It occurs to me that Wendy Hook sounds very good to the ear. It also occurs to me that I should meet your family and gain their blessing. What do you say to a trip to New London and a family reunion?"

Her heart skipped a beat. "I'd like to see my family again, but are you implying this visit's going to end with a proposal.? Do you expect me to become your little wife, Captain Hook?" She tried to sound put off by the idea, but couldn't stifle the grin that kept pushing through.

He chuckled. "I certainly do."

It was Wendy's turn to laugh. "I think

I'm the one who's supposed to say I do."

He leaned forward to kiss her nose. "No, you're supposed to say yes when I ask you to marry me, and then you say I do later, when we're standing in front of an officiant. Do you understand your orders, Ensign Darling?"

She grinned as she wiggled her bottom. "I'm not entirely sure, Captain. You might need to clarify."

Wendy couldn't hold in a giggle that was proof of pure joy as James pushed her back to the bed, pausing only long enough to contact Smee to alter their destination to New London before returning to her. He seemed determined to drive home his point, and she was more than happy to receive it over and over again as they crossed the lightyears separating them from New London, and the proposal waiting for her there.

She already knew exactly what she was going to say when he asked, and she was certain James did too. There was no holding back with him, and he wasn't shielding himself from her either. She would soon be his wife, and they would return to their quiet planet, but they wouldn't live a quiet life, by any means. It couldn't be any other way for a pirate captain and his adventurous wife-to-be.

1

ABOUT AURELIA

Aurelia Skye is the pen name *USA Today* bestselling author Kit Tunstall uses when writing science fiction romance. It's simply a way to separate the myriad types of stories she writes so readers know what to expect with each "author."

Made in the USA
Coppell, TX
23 March 2020